love, faith and a pair of pants

ALSO BY HERB FREED

Bashert

Herb Freed

love, faith and
a pair of pants

a novel in stories

BELLROCK PRESS   LOS ANGELES

Love, Faith and a Pair of Pants by Herb Freed
Published by Bellrock Press, Los Angeles, CA
Copyright © 2018 by Herb Freed

To reach the author or Bellrock Press email: bellrockpress@aol.com

ISBN: 978-0-9985339-2-6

Other available versions:
Hardcover—ISBN: 978-0-9985339-4-0
Digital Distribution—ISBN: 978-0-9985339-3-3

Manufactured in the United States of America
First Edition

Cover and book design by John Lotte
Author photo by Alan Weissman

For Marion

Sine Qua Non

CONTENTS

Reading Herb Freed's short stories about Rabbi Ben Zelig, I laughed and cried, from page to page. Once you start reading, you don't stop. Freed is a gifted story-teller with a vivid imagination and a wonderful power of narrative. He captures your attention and then seizes your heart and doesn't let go. He invents people you'd want to know, beginning with the rabbi himself. In these stories you meet the daughter of a great theologian of Judaism who dances in a strip club, an actress dying of cancer, a rabbi's first funeral and what can go wrong (more or less, everything). Someone shakes a finger at the young rabbinical student and warns, "If you become a Rabbi, you will delay the coming of the Messiah for another thousand years." The stakes in these stories mount up.

Each one of the stories takes up a classic theme of the Torah and translates it into a credible story, populated by real people. Ezekiel, Job, Ruth and Naomi all come on stage. Freed is a film director and writer and producer, as well as a rabbi, and he makes his characters live. The rabbi's mother chooses his wife in a reprise of the story of Ruth and Naomi. Freed has already shown how that has happened, then he spells it out—in the manner of Midrash—or film. But what else would you expect from the only member of the Director's Guild of America and the Writers Guild, west, who is also a member of the Rabbinical Assembly of America (Conservative Judaism).

Some writers use Judaism for color or texture. Freed doesn't do that, he sets out to imagine what "Judaism" would be like if its truths could be translated into the relationships of fathers and daughters, mothers and sons, the living and the dying, the healthy and the sick. And that is his starting point, an act of imagination that transforms biblical narratives into enchanting events of here and now. But Freed is never didactic. He doesn't preach. He makes his statement of Judaism through his stories. His complete success calls to mind the judgment of the great Catholic social scientist, Andrew M. Greeley, who writes, "Religion is story, story before it is anything else, story after it is everything else." In that context, Freed's book is an act of religion. It is not *about* Judaism, but it is a book of Judaism: it is a *sefer*.

Professor Jacob Neusner
A version of this foreword originally appeared in the *Jerusalem Post*.

the fatal flaw

1969.

THE TOP FLOOR of the Rabbinical Academy dormitory was the quietest place in Manhattan until six-fifteen in the morning when the clicking of high heels reverberated all the way down the marble-tiled hallway and woke Ben, just like it had every morning for the past two weeks. The main gate was locked from midnight until six, which was the earliest an overnight guest could leave. Ben waited until the clicking passed his door, and then opened it ever so slightly. As he watched, a heart-stopping knockout attempted to tiptoe gingerly down the hushed hallway past austere portraits of rabbis and scholars toward the elevator. Ben's heart skipped a beat.

She appeared to be walking in slow motion. Her rich sable hair with the Grace Kelly wave swayed gently across her neck. *How did Morty Kravitz ever get a beauty like that? Perfect waist, just the right height, not too tall,* Ben thought as she disappeared into the elevator. *Flawless!*

"WHERE DID YOU FIND that great-looking girl?" Ben asked Morty after the morning prayer service on their way to the breakfast room.

"Janice? She *is* a beauty and smart, too," Morty said as they sat down at the square porcelain table in the squeaky clean dining hall. "We met two weeks ago at a funeral, of all places." He rolled back the Saran Wrap from a cereal bowl.

"You hit on a mourner at a funeral?" Ben couldn't believe it.

"She hit on me," Morty smiled. "It was a funeral I was asked to conduct and the guy who died was some sort of uncle. He was apparently a miserable son of a bitch who everybody hated, so in my eulogy, I found a way to praise the guy without actually saying anything. After the burial, Janice introduced herself and said she was impressed by the way I eulogized the bastard—*her* word. She called it slight-of-mouth and said she thought I was hilarious."

"So, are you two going steady now?"

"More than that, Ben. I really like her. I think she just might be the one."

"How did you come to conduct a funeral? We don't graduate for another year and a half."

"The Intern Program," Morty said as he poured milk into his chocolate-flavored corn puffs. "I volunteered."

Ben knew about the program, which was created to give rabbinical students real-time experience with lay people, but considered it a waste of time since he hadn't yet decided whether he would assume a pulpit or teach at one of the Ivy League colleges. He leaned toward academia, but the rabbinate did have its attractions. Still . . . "Doesn't the Intern Program cut into your study time?"

"Not all that much," Morty said as he crunched his corn puffs. "It is definitely worth doing, especially if you're still trying to decide whether or not to take a pulpit. How else can you get a feeling for what life as a rabbi will be like? Classes at the Academy are stimulating, no doubt about that, but the best way to make a decision about how you want to spend the rest of your life is to interact with ordinary people who don't share our enthusiasm for Bible study, the Talmud, holidays and the rest. In the program you meet people you would never find at the Academy."

He's right, Ben thought. Getting to meet new people would be a major boost for him after ordination—and it might even be helpful now. Ben's social life was seriously stunted. When was the last time he went out on a date? He had to think. *Oh, yeah . . . Yuck!* Ben would love to meet new people—and who knows? He might even find a Janice.

That morning, Ben signed up for the Intern Program. He didn't hear anything for three weeks, then, finally, he received a call from Dean Warburg. Ben was assigned a funeral the following Sunday morning. He was given an address in Flushing on Long Island, where he could meet the family of the bereaved and learn how to best eulogize the deceased. This being Ben's first life-cycle event, the Dean advised him to wear a dark suit, conservative tie—and a hat. "Most lay people think the older a rabbi looks, the more he knows. A hat goes a long way," the Dean said. "Call me on Monday and let me know how it went. I'm sure you will be fine."

ON SATURDAY EVENING, Ben, attired in his dark gray, three-piece suit, white shirt, black and gray striped tie and the newly acquired Homburg, took three subway trains to Flushing, Queens, to meet the family—and check out the terrain.

The Zimmelman family greeted Ben warmly. There must have been twenty people crowded into the small living room with plastic-covered mohair chairs, oversized purple couch and folding chairs lining the walls. There were brothers, sisters-in-law and an endless number of children, grandchildren and cousins, all of whom were introduced by name, profession or business, and relation to the deceased. They inundated Ben with a plethora of details: where they lived, whose grandfather, mother or distant relative never missed a fast on Yom Kippur, and whose great-uncle was a famous rabbi somewhere in Europe. They seemed disappointed that Ben wasn't more enthusiastic about those revelations, but he was only half-listening as he searched for at least one good looking, available girl. The only one who might have aroused his interest was Sarah, one of the granddaughters. She was eager, friendly and fairly good looking, but alarmingly thin, and it wasn't just that. What killed it for Ben were her braces, upper *and* lower. When she smiled, they seemed to sparkle, reflecting the overhead light and that was just too weird.

"I'm sorry I never met Irwin," Ben said, getting down to business and trying his best to sound rabbinic. He sat down on an empty folding chair and pulled a yellow pad out of his briefcase. "I'd appreciate it if you could tell me about him."

"You want stories about Irwin, Rabbi?" Morris, the most forthcoming member of the extended family jumped in. "I got tons of 'em. Irwin Zimmelman was written up in books. Everybody knew him. Great man, brilliant." Heads nodded as Morris praised the deceased. "May he rest in peace," he said.

The crowd mumbled, ". . . rest in peace . . . *omeyn.*" Other members of the family pitched in, reminding one another of the Irwin they loved and who lived a full life.

Morris made sure his contribution would be referred to in the eulogy. "A saint, that's what Irwin was. The man was a saint, and you can quote me on that," he said, pointing to the yellow pad on Ben's lap. "Morris Brodsky is my name, with two Rs."

This was Ben's first experience preparing a eulogy and not knowing what might be important and what to leave out, he wrote down everything they said. "Did I understand you to say that Irwin was mentioned in some book?" Ben asked Morris.

"Some book? Tons, I'm telling you! The man was written up in all kinds of books." Morris shrugged. "I can't think of the names off hand, but look it up. You'll find Irwin Zimmelman everywhere." He thought for a moment. "I wish I could remember . . . it's hard when you get old."

"Okay," Ben said, reluctant to put Morris on the spot. "Can anybody tell me something *specific* about Irwin?"

Silence. Then, "He saved rubber bands," said the granddaughter, flashing her braces.

"And don't forget the small shopping bags from the supermarket," the girl's mother reminded her. "He always kept a huge stack of them under the sink."

"Why did he do that?" Ben asked.

"For the garbage," the granddaughter replied. "He always wrapped his garbage in neat little packages tied with rubber bands so the rats wouldn't make a mess when they put out the big cans on Wednesdays for the sanitation department pickup."

Glancing at his yellow pad, Ben wondered. *Why am I writing this stuff down? How do I construct a eulogy around rubber bands and garbage?* Ben looked at the well-meaning relatives. "Anything else beside the rubber bands and the garbage?"

"Uncle Irwin never let anyone near the dishwasher," a middle-age woman with a shiny black bouffant hairdo said proudly. "It was his favorite appliance. There is only one way to load a dishwasher, he always said . . ."

"The right way and the wrong way!" several of the guests chimed in unison.

Then the discussion shifted to how hard it is to find a place to park ever since Queens County introduced new alternate-side-of-the-street restrictions. "They'll cite you for a little nothing because the damn cops got to fill quotas! I'm telling you . . ." and Irwin was all but forgotten during the venting about corruption in city politics.

That was followed by a brief silence. Then came the jokes. "Did you hear the one about . . . ?"

THE FOLLOWING MORNING, Ben sat on a high-backed chair next to the lectern in The House of David Funeral Parlor, Central Queens Division. The huge, circular ceiling dwarfed the small group of mourners. A simple wooden coffin sat on a raised gurney bedecked with gray drapes. On a three-legged stand next to the coffin was an enlarged black and white photograph of young Irwin wearing a gray baseball cap that read South Shore Bombers and matching jersey, number 17. The family and friends assembled in the first few rows of the enormous room and when the crowd settled down, Ben rose to the lectern and opened with a recitation of the Twenty-Third Psalm. Barely halfway through, ". . . *Yea, though I walk through the valley of the shadow of . . ."* an old man with wild white hair stumbled into the room through the glass doors at the far end, screaming. "Oh my God, my kid brother Izzy is dead. Good natured Izzy, poor sweet boy. Why, God, why?"

A man in his seventies stood up in the front row. "Dave. I'm your brother Izzy. I'm not dead. I'm fine."

Dave looked at him. "Oh thank God you're alive, Izzy. I felt so terrible. Wait a minute. Then, who died?"

"Irwin."

Dave cupped his ear with one hand, to make sure he heard what he thought he had heard, and then screamed again. "Oh, God, no! My handsome brother Mervin is dead. Why God? Why?"

Another man in his seventies stood up next to Izzy. "Hey Dave, I'm your brother Mervin. I'm alive, see? I'm not handsome anymore but, otherwise, I'm fine."

Dave looked puzzled. "Then, who died?"

"Our brother-in-law *Irwin*," Mervin said. "Sarah's husband. He's the one who died."

"Irwin? That's all? Oh, thank God."

It went downhill from there.

When the crowd settled down, Ben proceeded to read from the *Rabbi's Manual*: "The grass withereth, the flower fadeth, but our love for Irwin endures . . ." When he looked up, and saw that no one was paying attention, Ben made a decision to liven up the service. He remembered a story he had heard the previous evening about how Irwin Zimmelman was the first Jew to move into the South Shore, which was then predominantly a gentile section of Long Island. That was a courageous thing to do in the 1940s and it paved the way for integration.

"There have always been pioneers among us," Ben said. He spoke of the *Halutzim*, the first wave of pioneers from

Europe who went to Palestine in the early years of the twentieth century. "They faced hostile enemies on all sides, but they fearlessly cleared the malaria-infested swamps to prepare a homeland for their brethren from the far corners of the earth." Ben wasn't sure how far to take the analogy, so he cut it short and went straight to Irwin Zimmelman, "who displayed the pioneer spirit required to be the first Jew to settle in Upper Islip, Long Island."

"Where did you hear that crap?" A man who couldn't be more than four feet tall, wearing a red flannel shirt under his green plaid sport jacket, stood up and demanded in a high-pitched voice. "I was the first one to move there with the Nazis."

"Be quiet Jake." Mervin and Izzy stood up and glared down at the very short man. Jake sat down but continued to talk just loud enough for everyone to hear that he was still bitching.

"Never mind him, Rabbi, go on," Izzy urged by way of apology.

Things were not going as Ben hoped, so he decided to return to the text and began to recite the *Kaddish* when a young girl of around nine or ten came to the podium and handed him a note from the family. Ben took it and read aloud. "Mervin's cousin Leonard is III." Unsure how to handle it, Ben added "Mazel tov, Leonard, on your one hundred and eleventh birthday."

There was an awful commotion. Mervin stood up and waved both hands. "Rabbi, Leonard isn't a hundred and eleven. My note said Cousin Leonard is ill. For two weeks now he's got laryngitis. You read it wrong."

"Why did you interrupt me in the middle of the *Kaddish*?"

"My sister Pearl says to me, as long as we're all here, for the same money, why not throw in a prayer for Leonard also?"

"The *Kaddish* is recited to honor the dead," Ben explained.

"If you go to any synagogue on the Sabbath, I'm sure they'll be happy to recite a prayer for Leonard."

Ben's nerves were rattled and his hands were shaking but Mervin seemed to enjoy the spotlight. "Everybody's here now," Mervin said, looking around at the small crowd. "Who knows what will be with Leonard?" He was now controlling the event. "Maybe he'll develop cancer of the throat,"

The woman next to him let out a shriek.

"I'm not saying he's going to die, Pearl," Mervin chastised. "All I'm saying is why not make the most of the occasion? Irwin is already dead, so nothing will help him anymore, but Leonard might get better tomorrow if we can stick in the right prayer, no? What can it hurt?"

"You're an idiot, Mervin," Pearl screamed. "How can you even . . ." and the two of them went at it.

What should Ben do to get this funeral back on track? He couldn't think of anything. Then, while Leonard and Pearl screamed at one another, the most amazing thing happened. At the rear entrance of the large room Ben saw what could only be a mirage. The most beautiful girl he had ever seen entered through the door on the left, behind rows of empty seats, and glided across the stone-tiled floor. She was an angel, a nymph in a black silk chiffon dress, waves of golden hair caressing her perfect face. Her full, luscious body reminded him of Bathsheba, the magnificent sculpture that excited Ben when he saw it at the Met, just last week. Ben was spellbound. Even the angry bickering in the front rows seemed to become less aggressive as the phantom beauty wafted across the room. When she reached the other side, she opened the door and disappeared.

"Go ahead, Rabbi," Mervin said, waving an angry hand at his sister. "Finish up."

Still in a trance, Ben quietly chanted the closing prayers without mentioning any specifics: not the dead, the sick or the brief moment of splendor.

After the burial, Ben looked for the quickest way to the subway. The service was a disaster. The only thing he allowed himself to think about was that fantastic incarnation of Bathsheba, who sailed across the back of the funeral home for a brief moment. Was she real?

As Ben walked down the narrow cemetery path searching for signs to the main exit, he heard someone call out. "Hey, Rabbi, wait up!" Ben looked around and saw a very large man with a face the shape of a pumpkin, and cauliflower ear, approaching him. He was dressed in a black suit, black shirt, white tie and a black snap-brim fedora with a red feather.

"I've known the Zimmelmans for years," the man said, catching his breath.

Who the hell cares? Ben wanted to say, but didn't. Instead, he said what he thought rabbis were supposed to say. "How interesting."

"Yeah it is. Irwin was a client of mine. We done business for years."

Ben had run out of things rabbis are supposed to say so he just stood there and looked at the very large man with the mangled ear and waited for him to stop talking.

He didn't stop. "I'll tell you something, Rabbi. You did a hell of a job considering you didn't know anybody and you're obviously still green around the edges."

Rabbis are definitely not supposed to tells *nudniks* to go to hell but Ben was getting ready to make an exception.

"Listen," Gargantua continued. "I wonder if you would do me a favor. My name is Katz, Seymour Katz. You can call me

Seymour. My mother is buried on the next hill. Maybe you could say a few words over her?"

"You mean, an *el maleh rachmim* prayer?"

"Yeah. Whatever."

A prayer is a prayer and even a *nudnik* can't be denied one. Ben followed Seymour over several grassy hills and stopped at a large tombstone.

"This is her," Seymour said, out of breath after the climb, then kissed the headstone.

Ben opened his *Rabbi's Manual* and began to chant the traditional *"El Moleh Rachim."* When it came to inserting the deceased's name, he turned to his companion.

"Theda Katzenelenson" he said, "like it says on the tombstone." He shook his head as if to say—*Can't you read?*

"No, what's her Hebrew name?" The stone bore only the English inscription.

"Her maiden name was Kugel. She's been dead for over for twenty years."

"Not her maiden name. What was her Hebrew name?"

"Theda, like the silent screen star, Theda Bara. Ah, you probably don't even know who she was. You're kind of young to be a rabbi, aincha?"

How could Ben retaliate? The reason he wore the dull gray Homburg was because he was told it would make him look older. Obviously, it didn't but Ben was too worn out to defend himself. All he wanted to do now was go back to the dorm and watch the Jets game on TV. It was obvious Seymour had no idea what his mother's Hebrew name was, so Ben inserted the name Thea, which means resurrection in Hebrew. For her father's name, which he also didn't know, Ben skipped a few millennia and addressed her as the daughter of Abraham, our patriarch. Seymour stood silently, head bowed and hands behind his back. Ben completed the prayer, said, "Amen," and closed his manual. "It is customary," he said "to make a charitable contribution in the name of the deceased."

"Don't worry about it" Seymour winked. He thanked Ben graciously and shook his hand. Ben started to say the formulaic, "It was nice to meet . . ." but stopped when he felt something crumbly in his hand. Seymour had slipped a twenty-dollar bill into his palm.

"This is not what I meant by charity," Ben said coldly.

"Buy a hat," Seymour winked again.

Ben could no longer restrain himself. Everything he did that day was wrong and he hated feeling like a total loser. Now this stranger was making him feel like a *schnorrer*.

"I have a hat!" Ben felt foolish enough wearing the stupid Homburg and the last thing he needed just then was Seymour's winking disapproval. "Where do you get off telling me what to wear? You asked me to do you a favor, which I'm happy to do, and you thank me by insulting me? I can't take money for offering a prayer!"

"Who's insulting? You never heard the expression, buy a hat? It's a New York thing. Where did you grow up, out west?"

"Ohio."

"Figures. In New York, 'buy a hat' is what you say when you want to give a guy a double sawbuck. You must have slang in Oklahoma, right? I'm giving you a friendly touch, rabbi. No reason to get all huffy."

"Take the money back," Ben glowered. "I'm not huffy, but I'll get angry as hell if you don't take it."

Seymour took the money and shrugged as if to say, *what a jerk.*

Ben felt like a jerk.

"So where's your congregation?"

"I don't have one. I'm still a student. I don't graduate until next year. Do you know how I can get the subway to Broadway and 116th?"

"Sure, come with me. I'm going as far as 57th Street. Follow the signs from there." They were on the I.R.T. heading into Manhattan for about twenty minutes before either of them spoke. Given the trouble it took to be heard on the subway, Ben didn't bother trying to talk. He had nothing to say.

Seymour Katz did. "How old did you say you were?"

"What is this obsession with my age?"

"Why are you so defensive? I'm being friendly. So, are you single?"

"Yes."

"Why is that?"

"Because I'm not married."

"Are you interested in getting married?"

"Are you proposing?"

Seymour laughed. "For a rabbi, you got a hell of a sense of humor." After slapping his thigh, he looked at Ben again. "The reason I'm asking is, I know a young girl, the daughter of a close friend of mine. She is absolutely gorgeous, smart, a college graduate and not just any college, but one of those fancy schools around Boston."

Ben had no response, which Seymour chose to interpret as a sign that he was interested. "Now here's the beauty part. Her father is a banker, money up the kazoo."

"Who do you want to fix me up with, the girl or her father?"

Seymour laughed out loud again. "I swear to God, for a hick you got a real funny bone. So, you're interested, right?"

What could Ben say? If a friend offered to fix him up, he would ask a question or two and call the girl. But a guy he just met at a cemetery, who happens to be the ugliest man he ever saw and someone he already doesn't like? Ben frowned as he tried to think of a graceful way out.

"What are you thinking so hard about? Like I asked you to smell a chicken's ass to see if it's kosher like my mother used to ask her rabbi? This girl I'm talking about is a stunner. She dresses classy and she's funny. You got something against smart, good looking, young girls?"

"So what's wrong with her?" Ben asked. "Does she limp a little but you don't notice it when she sits?" he said, referring to the old joke.

"What limp? She's a dancer, studied with Martha Graham for years; performed with the chorus at the Met when she was twelve. Limp? Hell, a pair of gams she's got on her, you don't see every day. If you want to know what's the problem, I'll tell you plain out. She don't know many Jewish boys and her father doesn't want her going out with *goyim*, so everybody's unhappy. Why am I talking to you? Because you're a nice Jewish boy; plus, I owe you one. So if it should happen to click, I'm doin' my friends a favor, and you, since you won't accept my double sawbuck, I'm giving an opportunity to go out on a date with a real cutie. I figure that will even the score between us. Is that so terrible?"

"So—what *is* her fatal flaw?"

Now Seymour was offended. "I'm talking a perfect girl here. What are you looking for flaws?"

"Look, Mr. Katz . . ."

"Seymour."

"Seymour, I'm not *looking* for flaws, but every time somebody talks to me about 'a perfect girl' it always ends up being somebody with a whole series of flaws, at least one of which is fatal."

Seymour smiled. "Not this one. I swear on the prayer you

recited over my dead mother, rest her soul. This girl is closer to perfect than anybody you'll ever meet if you live to be a hundred. Look, the worst that can happen is you call her up, take her to a movie or better yet, go dancing. She loves to dance. Oh, I guess being a rabbi and all, you don't dance, but maybe she can teach you."

"Of course I dance. I've danced all my life. Most rabbis I know dance." Ben fumed. *No matter what course the conversation takes, this guy finds ways to insult me!*

"Oh, yeah? I did not know that."

Ben was dying to tell him he didn't know shit. Instead, he pressed the back of his hand against his lips as if afraid the words would escape.

"So, you gonna call her or what?"

"Who is this flawless girl, a relative of yours?" Ben said, looking at Seymour's huge, ugly head and trying to imagine what this *cutie* could possibly look like.

"Her name is Cynthia and no, we're not related. She's my boss's daughter and I've known her most of her life. Come on, you're not married. I never heard of a queer rabbi, so what's the problem? Are you engaged?

"No."

"A steady girl?"

Ben said nothing, but Seymour could tell he didn't have that either. He took out a small pad, wrote down a name and number and stuffed the sheet he ripped off into Ben's jacket pocket.

"What's your number?" Seymour held his pen at the ready.

"Riverside 5-9979" How could Ben not give it to him?

"What's that, an office?"

"It's the switchboard in my dorm," Ben said. They'll ring me."

"Who do I ask for?"

"Ben Zelig. Uh, Intern Rabbi Ben Zelig." *This guy doesn't even know my name,* Ben bristled, *and I'm going to let him fix me up?*

As Ben left the train at the 116th Street station, he tossed the note into a trash bin.

Over the ensuing days, the more Ben thought about Seymour Katz the angrier he got. The arrogance. The effrontery. There was nothing about him that Ben liked. He was tactless and crude. *How could he possibly know the kind of girl I would want to meet?* Ben's irritation increased, more with himself for not responding aggressively to that jerk, but as an *Intern Rabbi,* he had no idea how he was supposed to act when someone pissed him off. Ben compiled a list of barbed retorts to nail him when he called, but after three weeks passed and he didn't hear from Seymour, Ben's annoyance slowly disappeared and, in a perverse way, he actually missed the man.

BEN SHOULD HAVE BEEN ABLE to sleep better now that Morty Kravitz moved out of the dorm to live with Janice, but that didn't happen. Every morning, Ben got up at a quarter past six and thought about Morty who found a beautiful girl *who just might be the one* and the sting was even sharper now. His loneliness was taking over and he actually began to think that he may have acted too hastily when Seymour offered to fix him up with a date. He knew that this girl could not possibly be who he was looking for, but at least he wouldn't feel so miserably alone.

Just then, a street repair crew started to drill outside Ben's window. Before he could close it, the phone rang. Ben picked it up but it was hard to hear with all the noise from the street.

"Howya doin', Rabbi? Betcha thought I forgot about you."

"Who is this?" Ben asked, but he knew immediately that it was Seymour Katz and his heart began to race. *I wonder if he's going to try and dump his friend's daughter on me again. What do I say? Am I more irritated than I am lonely? Hell no, but I don't want to sound too anxious, either.*

Before Ben could decide, Seymour slapped him down again. "Boy, for a rabbi, you're not the brightest star in the sky. How could you forget so soon? It's me, Seymour. Listen, you remember the girl I told you about?"

"How could I forget the 'flawless' girl? Father's a banker as I recall."

"Also from a long line of famous Jews, did I tell you that? Listen, I told my friend about you. He keeps his daughter pretty much housebound because he doesn't want her going out with just any *schmuck*, but when I told him you were a rabbi, well almost a rabbi, he's willing to make an exception. Her name is Cynthia, which you probably forgot since you obviously never got around to calling her. So listen, she has long blonde hair, an hourglass figure and the face of an angel. She'll pick you up on the southwest corner of 113th Street and Broadway at eight o'clock tonight. Look for a gorgeous girl in a black Corvette."

"Whoa! I'm not sure. I may be . . . uh . . . how do you know I live on 113th Street and Broadway?"

"Eight o'clock. Sharp! Southwest corner. Black Corvette. And Rabbi, don't wear that silly hat."

Ben hung up and smoldered. How does he know where I live? How dare he! Then Ben thought about the long blonde hair, the hourglass figure, the face of—an angel?

Ben waited on the corner for over an hour, getting angrier

by the minute for allowing himself to be sucked in again. At a quarter past nine he was about to go home when a black Corvette convertible pulled up.

"You the rabbi?" A girl's voice called from the driver's seat.

As Ben approached the car, he couldn't help but notice the beautiful face of the Bathsheba who floated by during the funeral.

"You're Cynthia?" he asked cautiously. He couldn't believe his luck.

"Get in." A smile lit up her perfect face.

It took Ben a moment to catch his breath. Never having been in a Corvette, he was unprepared for the contortions required by the low frame. He stumbled, climbing in. She smiled as Ben clumsily struggled with the slung-back bucket seat. He hoped he didn't look too awkward.

"For a rabbi, you're quite a hunk," she said with a teasing smile.

Ben blushed. She laughed, put the car in gear and gunned the motor.

So many things were flashing through his mind. Here he was, on a date with the most tantalizing beauty he ever saw! He studied every inch of her captivating face, her soft blue eyes, smooth skin. She was beyond flawless. She was sublime.

"I didn't mean to embarrass you. Sorry if I did, Rabbi."

"I'm not really a rabbi," Ben said. Not yet, that is."

"But you will be?"

"Not if it makes me less of a hunk. Call me Ben."

She laughed again. "Ben, I like your priorities. You okay with the top down?"

"The only way to ride in a Corvette—provided it's a convertible."

Her warm, easy smile at his lame joke made Ben feel comfortably at home as they drove.

"When do you become a real rabbi?"

"I graduate next year, but I haven't decided whether I'm going to continue in the rabbinate or not."

"What's the alternative?"

"I'm not really sure. Maybe academia, but to be perfectly honest, I have no idea."

"Oh, that magic feeling, nowhere to go," she said, as though she were reminding herself.

"Abbey Road! That's one of my favorite lyrics," Ben said. It suddenly struck him. "That *magic* feeling—nowhere to go." What a smart girl. I'll have to remember to use that in my class paper, he thought, making a mental note.

Cynthia talked about Abbey Road, The Beatles and the blending of folk with jazz in Wilson Pickett's version of "Hey, Jude" and the impact that had on The Rolling Stones. Everything she said was spontaneous and smart!

"Am I boring you?" she asked sweetly.

"Are you kidding?" *I can't get enough of you.* Ben didn't have the guts to say it aloud. "Please continue," was the best he could do.

She was driving towards the Village but Ben didn't care if they actually went anywhere. He just wanted to be with her, look at her and listen to her. What a treasure. What a face—and the sweetest smile.

"Tell me about you," she turned to Ben. "How are you dealing with the existential angst?"

"Badly, I'm afraid."

"But if you don't become a rabbi after all that training, what are you going to do with your life?"

"I didn't say I was not going into the rabbinate. The truth is, I can't seem to make up my mind."

"You're obviously contemplating some pretty radical changes. That's a scary place to be, not to mention lonely."

This girl tuned into Ben's wavelength like no one else ever had. She said it all. She couldn't have chosen two more appropriate words to sum up his dilemma: "Scary and lonely."

"On the other hand," she said, "*angst* is a double-edged emotion. Making choices for the rest of your life is a heavy burden, but having the power to make those choices can give you that special exhilaration that only comes with the freedom to choose."

My God, she's quoting Kierkegaard! How many girls has he ever met who even know who Kierkegaard was?

"Unless . . ." she was somewhere deep inside her own head, ". . . unless Kierkegaard lied about the special exhilaration and he only said that to make the burden more bearable."

"I hope that's not true," Ben said. "I'm badly in need of some exhilaration because for the most part I'm stuck between scary and lonely."

"You'll survive," she said sadly. "Everybody does. You're not alone, you know. Most people continue to make major changes throughout their lives. I certainly do."

"Is it too soon to ask what kinds of changes you're going through?" Ben asked

"Yes," Cynthia said. Her tone was so solemn Ben knew he had better slow down.

They didn't talk for the next few blocks. Finally, Ben said "It was nice of Mr. Katz to fix us up."

"Who?"

"Seymour Katz?"

"Oh, Uncle See," she laughed.

"He's your uncle?"

"No, just an old friend, but I've known him since I was child. He's worked for my father for years."

"Seymour said your father was a banker."

"I guess you could say that," Cynthia said without looking at Ben. "Dad's a loan shark. Uncle See used to be one of his enforcers."

Ben was suddenly bombarded by new sensations. Could he really get serious about the daughter of a gangster? Ah, so there's the flaw. He had to pause a moment to let that sink in. *I wouldn't be marrying the father*, he reasoned. Ben was silent for a few minutes, sorting all this out as they drove through the Village. "Are we going somewhere in particular?" he asked. "I heard you like to dance and I know a place near here I think you'd like."

"Hmm," she said, obviously not interested, but he didn't mind. He was soaring on the wings of an angel. This was a totally new experience for Ben. Whenever something seemed too good to be true, it always ended up being just that. But where was her fatal flaw? If her only drawback was her father, he could live with that.

The Corvette pulled up in front of a gaudily lit club on Greenwich Avenue called La Cucaracha. Cynthia looked Ben over. "You might want to take off your jacket and tie. This is a pretty casual place."

Without thinking, Ben took off his jacket and tie and looked for a place to put them.

"Toss them behind the seat," she said.

Ben had never been in a Corvette and was unaware that there was an open space behind the tight-fitting bucket seats.

"Maybe the shirt, too," she added.

Ben thought for a second. Could he be sure he was wearing

an undershirt that didn't have holes in it? Not worth the risk. "I'm good," he said.

Cynthia slipped the Corvette into an impossibly small space with astonishing ease. Ben didn't know if he should applaud her deftness or just take it in stride. Either way, the only thing to do was get out. It wasn't the easiest car to climb out of, but he pulled himself up and tucked the shirttails into his trousers. When he saw Cynthia's lovely form come around the car, he quickly took her extended hand. In a shocking moment, his rapture quickly dimmed. A tremor went through him when he saw that three fingers were missing from Cynthia's disfigured left hand. How could he not have noticed it?

"I guess Uncle See didn't tell you about my hand." There was no way for her not to see the shocked look on Ben's face.

"Sure he did" Ben tried to pretend. "An accident, right?"

"Congenital. I've lived with it all my life so it's no big deal for me, but it is for some people. You can leave now if you're uncomfortable." She pulled her hand away and walked towards the darkened doors that were covered with a version of Andy Warhol's soup cans.

Ben caught up with her before she reached the doors. "Cynthia, I think you're great and I'm the luckiest guy in the world to be with you tonight."

She looked at him for a long moment then flashed the sweetest smile and touched his face with her good hand. *It felt like velvet.*

As soon as they walked through the door they were hit by a wave of brassy salsa music and momentarily blinded by a circling band of colors from a light wheel. As Ben followed her through the crowd, he felt immensely satisfied with himself. He had discovered her flaw and he could deal with that.

As they walked into La Cucaracha Ben wondered if there

was some dress code or theme. One bare-chested man in full cowboy regalia with hat, vest and leather chaps, kept his hand on a holstered six-shooter that dangled between his legs. Several men—and perhaps women—wore motorcycle gear. One elaborately dressed woman in high heels with a sumptuous hair-do, smiled invitingly at Dan. As she danced, her tight dress revealed a hairy chest. Ben returned the smile and quickly looked away.

As they pushed their way across the dance floor, Ben tried not to stare at the couples alternately leaping and swaying, particularly as girls were holding girls and guys had their arms wrapped around other guys. This was his first experience in what looked like a gay bar and he was determined to appear cool.

On stage, a girl with wild red hair held a microphone in her hand and goaded the audience between verses of a song that was as hot as the lyrics were unintelligible. "Who's got the better voice, Eydie Gormé or Dusty?" she taunted a heckler at the bar in a T-shirt that Ben couldn't read because a big white question mark was painted over the words. Cynthia waved to the girl on stage whose accent was so thick, it was hard to tell where it came from. Whatever her origin, she held the crowd in the palm of her hand.

When she saw Cynthia, she blew a kiss and mouthed something Ben didn't get. It seemed from the cheering crowd that her name was "Magdalena." Her blouse was cut low, high-lighting well-shaped breasts. As Ben's eyes adjusted to the spinning light, he saw that the girl on stage was really a beauty.

"Dusty man! Eydie Gormé ain't shit." The heckler of indeterminate age and sex turned to an equally ambiguous blond youth; they elbowed one another then kissed.

Magdalena got up from her stool and looked at the two hecklers.

"What is it wit youse two *maricons*? You on your honeymoon or what? Go out to the parking lot fer chrissakes, or at least, the bathroom."

Ben watched Cynthia's face as she swayed to the earsplitting music and he was struck with a revelation. This raucous bar was a surreal extension of the racket outside his window earlier when Seymour called. It was all pre-ordained. Through the cacophonous weirdness, Leonard Cohen's soft clear voice emerged from some distant place in Ben's soul. *". . . there is a crack, a crack in everything. That's how the light comes in, that's how the light comes in."* Ben felt himself seeing, hearing, and feeling more clearly than he had in years.

The music came up full again and the crowd howled as Magdalena began to spin with the frenzy of a dervish. The bar was steamy, boisterous and dark except for the brutal flashes of garish lights, but the music was intoxicating. Everyone in the bar seemed to be regulars: every race seemed to be represented in endless combinations.

Someone poked Ben on the arm. He wasn't sure if the person at the bar wearing a black-and-white snap brimmed hat, was talking to him until he was poked again. "Who's the 'ho'?" the androgynous individual asked, pointing a tiny finger at Cynthia.

"My wife." Ben had no idea why he said that, but it felt good to hear himself say it.

The pipsqueak turned to his companion wearing the same hat in reversed colors. *"Maricon* brings his wife to a placed like this. What an *esse.*"

Magdalena started to sing again and she was amazing. Ben didn't get the Spanglish-sounding lyrics, but the rest of the bar did and they cheered her on. Her body undulated to the syncopated rhythm of the drums and her chesty voice filled every crevice of the surreal place. Ben had never seen such erotic movements. There was a refrain that everyone seemed to know and they all joined in. Cynthia's face glowed as she sang along and Ben suddenly felt joyous and safe, protected by his divinely sent guide. He joined in, mouthing half-words that sounded right, at least in his head. When Magdalena finished the song, everyone was on their feet cheering, applauding, whistling and shouting words Dan didn't recognize, but it didn't matter because everybody else did. As soon as she finished, Magdalena made her way towards them.

"You're incredibly talented . . ." Ben started to say, but she wasn't listening. The music had picked up again full blast. She smiled conspiratorially at Cynthia, then, without a word, they joined arms and started to rock in perfect rhythm, locked in an exotic dance. They spun and twirled, their eyes riveted on one another like gypsies in a flamenco brawl. Their bodies glided and swayed through sensuous rhythms. The music ended on a triumphant note and Cynthia and Magdalena looked at each other for a long moment, and then kissed passionately. Ben was confused and excited. He wanted desperately to enter the erotic bubble that had engulfed the two women, but didn't know how.

After the long embrace, Magdalena looked at Ben "Who's the beard?" she asked.

Cynthia smiled sweetly at Ben and touched his face tenderly with her mangled hand. "His name is Ben. He's a rabbi."

"A rabbi? No shit!" Magdalena looked slyly at Cynthia. "So that's how you got your old man to let you out." Ben couldn't place her accent.

"Ben, this is Madge. They call her Magdalena here."

"I think you're incredibly talented," Ben said again, when suddenly the tone in the bar changed. Everyone was looking at the open Andy Warhol soup-can doors. An old *Chasid* with a long white beard, black coat and wide-brimmed hat stood in the doorway trying to adjust to the flashing lights. As he entered the bar, the *Chasid* passed beneath the light wheel, turning red, then blue, then yellow. Onlookers raucously heckled the gefilte fish out of water. The old man strained to see through the smoke, bombarded by flashes of violent lights. Blaring salsa music pierced the ears. As he approached, Ben panicked. *He must be looking for me. Why else would an old Chasid come to a place like this?* The *Chasid* pushed through the gyrating forms on the dance floor. The patrons shoved back and teased him.

"*Ola esse!*"

"Watch where you're goin'!"

"Hey, check out this *maricon*, man."

"Which one of you *muthas* forgot to pay the rent?" One of the dancers called out and the crowd around him cackled.

Amid the crescendo of catcalls, the bearded man finally stopped a few feet from Ben. "I'd like to explain . . ." Ben began, but stopped when he saw the *Chasid* take Magdalena's hand.

"*Kum aheim, tay-ere.*" The man said in Yiddish.

"Go home, Papa." Magdalena said softly. Suddenly, her accent was gone and Magdalena became Madge or possibly Miriam.

"I will not leave without you. *Dine mama challisht avek,*" the old man said.

"*Farshteys du noch nicht?* I can't be in the same room with her!" Madge tried to keep her voice down, but she was losing control.

"Your mother loves you, *tay-ere.*"

"She hates me, Papa. She's always hated me. I can't live with her another minute."

"So this is where you live now?" The old man looked around at the amazed faces. "With these animals?"

A short, tattooed girl wearing a black and white jump suit with the label, *New York Women's Detention Facility* grabbed the old man's collar. "Who you callin' animals, *maricon*?"

"Back off!" Madge screamed. The intruder stepped back immediately and the place became deathly still. Even the music stopped. The ground had shifted and no one was sure where they were.

Madge kissed Cynthia on the cheek. "I got to go, Cyn."

The old *Chasid* shifted his eyes to Ben. *Why is he looking at me?* Ben wondered. Was it because he was the only one who wasn't wearing something outlandish or exposing some part of his body? Or was it something else?

"Who are you?" the old man asked softly.

"Ben," he replied, his voice weak.

The *Chasid* leaned forward, his intense sad eyes trying to understand. He cupped his ear with one hand. "You don't got a name?"

Ben didn't know how or why it came out, but the words flowed from the depths of his soul. "I am Benjamin, son of Solomon, of the tribe of Levi," he said proudly.

Shocked, the *Chasid* stared at Ben. "You're a Jew?" He squinted as he studied his face.

"*Ivri anochi.*" Ben said, proudly quoting biblical Jonah verbatim in Hebrew. "I am a Hebrew and I worship the God of heaven and earth, who made the sea and the dry land."

"Where did you learn that?" the old man snapped, angrily.

"I am a rabbinical student," Ben said proudly, looking at Cynthia. "Next year, I will be a fully ordained rabbi."

The old man's mouth dropped. He reached up and touched

Ben's head. He was not wearing a *yarmulke*. The man's face twisted in anger as he pointed a shaking finger at Ben.

"No" he shrieked. "You must not become a rabbi! If you do, you will delay the coming of the Messiah for another thousand years."

Madge grabbed the old man's arm and led him away. The shocked spectators gave them a wide berth. When they reached the door, Madge turned back and waved to Cynthia. "Call me!"

Ben felt wounded. *Why did he say that?*

Cynthia looked at Ben tenderly for a long moment. Much as he wanted to, Ben couldn't let himself engage her eyes. It's not that he *believed* he was personally responsible for delaying the coming of the Messiah—at least he hoped he wasn't—but the words hung in the air and reminded him that his soul was in transit. Cynthia slowly wrapped her arms around him. It was like being anointed. Magically, in her embrace Ben felt the sludge that had begun to form around his brain, drain away. Cynthia had the power to lead him on the right path, he was convinced of that. They remained locked in that embrace. Suddenly, Ben felt he had to kiss her. He tried, but she turned away. He tried again—and again. Finally, she dropped her embrace and the music died.

ON THE DRIVE BACK, they didn't say a word. Ben looked at Cynthia several times but her eyes were glued to the road. When she stopped at the corner of 113th Street and Broadway, he slowly opened the door and got out, but couldn't leave. "Should I call you sometime?" was all he could say.

Cynthia looked at Ben and he saw a tear roll down her cheek. She brushed it away with the thumb and only finger of her deformed hand. "I think you'll be a fine rabbi, Ben, if that's what you want," she said softly. "You're a beautiful man." She wiped away more tears. Ben slowly shut the car door and in an instant she was gone.

A soft rain began to fall. As it increased, Ben felt he was Adam banished from the garden. Where to go from here?

The downpour became torrential and soon he was drenched. Just then, a truck drove by and hit a deep puddle, splashing muddy water all over him. Ben wanted to leave, to go somewhere, but where? He stood in the rain, rooted to the spot. His wet clothes felt warm and he was waiting to be born. More cars splashed him and people ran by bumping him with umbrellas, but he couldn't move.

Finally the rain stopped. Without thinking, Ben reached into his pocket and took out a *yarmulke*. He placed it on his head and began the long walk back to the Academy.

and a pair of pants

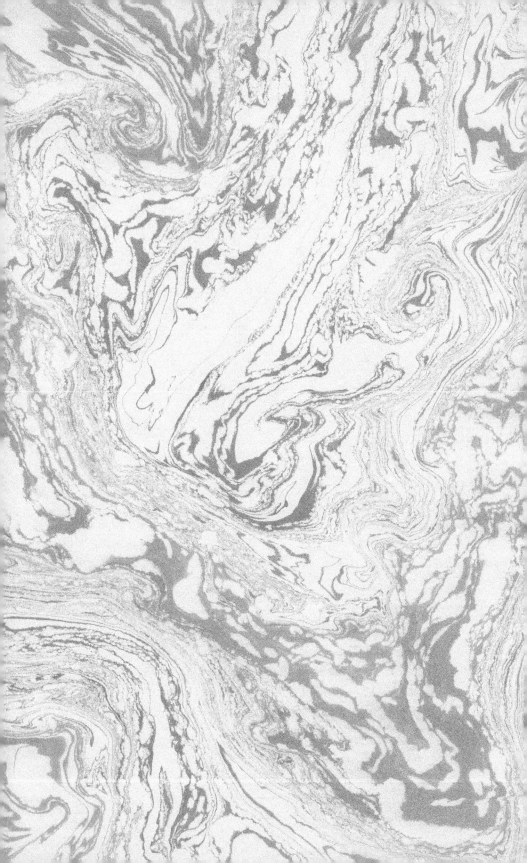

1970.

A MONTH BEFORE GRADUATION, Ben developed a severe case of hives. His life was about to undergo cataclysmic changes. There would be no more casual afternoons at The Museum of Modern Art debating Larry Rivers' outrageous takes on Michelangelo to impress Barnard girls wearing breathtakingly short plaid skirts and Go-go boots. No more evenings in the Village with kindred spirits, men with odd facial hair configurations and sexy girls in black leotards and matching eye shadow, drinking cheap wine and raging against "the regime." Goodbye, Bleeker Street. No more Bitter End and clicking fingers as Pete Seeger rowed his boat ashore on hootenanny nights. Instead, Ben would be expected to assume the duties of a practicing rabbi, comforting the sick, consoling the bereaved and nagging a reluctant flock to apply religious values to life in a secular world. The demands would be endless!

WITH EACH PASSING DAY, his hives itched more and more. "What are my options?" He asked himself. He had no other skills. Why hadn't he acquired any? With graduation approaching, the pressure mounted. Two weeks before ordination ceremonies, Ben, badly in need of a break, flew to Youngstown to spend the Shavuot holiday with his mother.

Ben's Uncle Joe, the only member of his family who was both a millionaire and illiterate, picked him up at the small airport with the dirt runway and yellow windsock between Akron and Youngstown. He seemed preoccupied as Ben followed him to the parking area. When they reached Uncle Joe's new, but unwashed, black Cadillac Eldorado, he opened his trunk. Ben watched the lid rise on the sleek machine then tucked his small leather suitcase between a crate of salamis and a carton of Tam-Tams.

Uncle Joe was uncharacteristically quiet as he closed the trunk. "So how are things in Youngstown?" Ben asked. Ignoring the question, Uncle Joe tugged his tie loose, took off the gray zippered sweater he wore year-round, and threw it onto the spacious white leather back seat. That's strange, Ben thought. Uncle Joe, the talking machine never missed an opportunity to answer a question whether he knew the answer or not. Joe turned on the ignition, backed the car out slowly and inched his way toward the exit, but still didn't say a word. Ben began to feel anxious.

"Is something wrong? Is Mom okay?" he asked.

Joe remained silent until they were out of the parking lot and onto the four-lane highway. Then the silence exploded into an all-out assault. "You want to know what's wrong?" Uncle Joe bellowed. "I'll tell you what's wrong. You! Dat's what's wrong. What de hell's de mattah wit' you Benny? Your mudda says you're t'inking about quitting the rabbi business before you even start! Whaddaya gonna do? Woik in a shoe store? Hold up a bank, maybe? You got yourself a respectable profession and you're akshally t'inkin' about t'rowin' it away? Dis ain't Europe! In de old country, a rabbi didn't have a pot to piss in. It's different in America. Here, a rabbi can make a damn good livin'! And you're gonna give dat up? Whaddaya, *meshuggah* altogedder?"

Ben winced. How could he explain his conundrum to his uncultivated uncle? Ben had spent his college and post-graduate years studying with some of the most erudite and saintly men in the world, many of whom were rescued from the camps and ovens of occupied Europe and brought to the Academy to ignite the spark of Jewish scholarship and commitment.

"Uncle Joe," he retorted, "those years at the Rabbinical Academy were dedicated to scholarship and the study of Torah. They were not spent preparing me to make 'a damn good livin'.'"

"Eh!" It was Uncle Joe's way of dismissing any argument that didn't have a cash equivalent. Then he cut loose. "What some people call a scholar, odder people call a *schnorrer,* a bum. I don't understand you, Benny. You're supposed to be smart. Your mudda says you know de whole Torah by heart. Please explain to me, Mr. Smart-feller-who-knows-de-whole-Torah-by-heart, what's wrong wit' practicing a profession where you can earn a dolla'?"

Ben quoted the Talmud. "One should not use the study of God's word to enrich himself." He had become adept at wrapping a protective shield of sanctified rabbinic maxims whenever he was challenged, but had he really been smart, he would have known that wouldn't work with Uncle Joe.

"Who's talkin' rich? I'm talkin' payin' your bills so you won't live like a dog in de street. Listen Benny, de reason I'm wasting my time talking to you is because I believe you are a smart boy and I hate to see you slide down de toilet. I'm telling you *emes,* true. You got de goods—and you will be a big hit as a rabbi. I know. I heard plenty rabbis in my time. Only a few of dem knew how to sell de goods. Most of dem put you right to sleep. But you, Benny," He pointed a finger at Ben and winked. "You! I heard you talk from de *bimah* on Passover when de rabbi invited you up. You're a natural born salesman. I never fell asleep on you once."

"Please, Uncle Joe. With all due respect, I am not a salesman. I don't know a thing about selling and I don't want to know."

"Excuse me, Mister Almost-Rabbi, but you're full of shit. Believe me; you know how to sell de goods."

Ben frowned.

"You're giving me a face? Why not listen to what I'm tellin' you instead? You might learn somet'ing. When somebody wants to buy a shirt in one of my shops and I sell 'em, you think dat makes me a salesman? No! Any clerk can sell somet'ing off de shelf. So, what's a salesman? Maybe somebody who sells you somet'ing you don't want? No! Lots of people can talk a fella into buying de next best t'ing. You want to know what's a salesman? I'll tell you. Det's de man who can sell you somet'ing you don't want, det he don't even have!"

Ben had no idea what Uncle Joe was talking about. How

does a person sell something he doesn't have? It sounded more complicated than calculus. Ben's frown deepened.

Uncle Joe flashed a triumphant smile. He knew precisely what he was talking about and he enjoyed the fact that someone with Ben's education couldn't follow him.

"I'm not surprised you don't understand," Uncle Joe said. "What I'm talking about isn't in any of your books."

This was a different Uncle Joe from the ignoramus who was scorned by the more educated members of Ben's family. He knew things they didn't and he was about to reveal them to Ben.

"Why does de man who sells you what you don't want, that he don't have, become a huge success? Because he is not selling moichandise. He's selling ideas. He understands human nature. He knows what a person would really like to buy and that's what he sells him. He understands that de sale is de thing, not de goods. Once you make de sale, it's no big deal to go out and find an acceptable product to deliver whether it's a motorcycle or a house. De best salesman is not de one wit' de big store. It's de man who can t'ink big."

Uncle Joe was a philosopher!

"Looky, here," he went on. "I can't tell you what it takes to be a good salesman with big words because I nevah had de opportunity to go to schools like you did, but I know what I know, so let me try to explain you anodder way."

With his thumbnail, Uncle Joe drew some lines in the dust on his dashboard. His Eldorado was just under a year old, but he never spent money to have it washed. He wasn't just saving money. The dust on his dashboard was where he did his calculating. "What kind of place you live in at that college? A hotel? A house?"

"After three years in the dormitory, I finally found a six-story walk-up on 111th street and Broadway that I share with three other guys. One goes to Juilliard, that's a music school in the area, and the other two are grad students at Columbia."

"How many students in all dem schools around dere?"

"I don't know. Between Union Theological, that's the largest Protestant Seminary in the country, the Rabbinical Academy, Juilliard, Barnard College and of course, Columbia, I would guess around thirty, forty thousand students a year, maybe more."

"They all got a place where to stay at?"

"Affordable rooms are scarce. My place is a dump and I was lucky to find it. As shabby as it is, it's better than the dorm. At lest I can come and go as I please."

"How many rooms in dis dump where you live at?"

"Four bedrooms, a kitchen and a bathroom."

"Rent is how much?"

"Three-hundred dollars a month. We all pay a quarter."

"How many apartments in de building?"

Ben told him. Joe thought for a moment, and then made some scratches in the dust on his dashboard.

"Here's what you'll do. You'll buy de building and sub-divide. You'll rent out each one-room apartment for twenty-five dollahs a week. Even students can afford twenty-five dollahs a week, no?"

"You're missing the point, Uncle Joe. There is no way . . ."

"Please shut your mouth for one minute. I'm trying to teach you somet'ing here, so listen with your ears for a change and stop making wit' de stupid interruptions. You're a smart boy, Benny, so just hear what I got to say. After det, if you got somet'ing worth saying, you can talk. But listen foist, okay?"

Ben swallowed a retort. "Okay."

"Now, all your tenants share one bathroom and one kitchen, so you got no new plumbing expenses."

"Yes, but . . ."

"Again with the mouth? I thought you was gonna listen with the ears first."

"Okay."

"Boy, it's hard to teach intallekshals t'ings that ain't in books." He shook his head and then went back to scratching in the dust of his dashboard. "So, you'll collect twenty-five dollahs for each room, det's a hundred dollahs a week. Det gives you four hundred dollahs a month. You got yourself a t'irty-t'ree and a t'ird, nearly t'irty-four per cent increase over what de guy makes who owns de building now. Good, no?"

"Good," Ben grunted. He didn't want to be told to "shut up" and he certainly wasn't eager to be called stupid again.

"Now, you'll raise de rent say, three, maybe five percent a year. Dere is five floors wit' two apartments on each floor. Det comes to . . ."

Ben's head was swimming and he had shooting pains in both temples. "Uncle Joe, please! Where would I get the money to buy a building even if I wanted to, which I don't?"

"Any bank would be happy to loan you money wit' an idea like det. You can write your own ticket. You'll get a t'irty-year mortgage wit' low interest, I'll betcha."

"You think I want to spend the next thirty years of my life paying off a loan for a building I don't want?"

"No, of course not! You never pay back a loan. When de bank sees how good yer doin', dey'll give you annoder loan to buy annoder building, maybe two. You'll be making money hand over fist."

When Uncle Joe saw how gloomy all this was making Ben,

he relented. "Benny, do you understand why I'm telling you dis? I'm not saying you should sell real estate. I know det's not for you. I'm only trying to explain to you det success in life depends not on what you stock in your shop, but what you got in your noggin." Uncle Joe knocked his knuckles against the side of Ben's head as he drove through a red light.

Ben clutched the armrest. "Uncle Joe, you just went through a red light!"

"You say it was red, I say yellow. Who should I believe? Anyhow, dis is important, so listen to what I'm telling you. I seen a painting a few years ago, maybe you seen it too. Some Dutch guy had an idea to paint a picture of an old pair of torn pants and *farkakte* wooden shoes. Now everybody sees bums in de street wit' *drek* on their cuffs every day, but nobody knows what they're lookin' at until dis one smart Dutchman paints det picture. When you see dem holes in de knees and de crusted cowshit on de cuffs and de broken down shoes, you suddenly understand how dis poor son of a bitch lived his whole life. I'm sure he sold dat picture for a pretty penny believe you me.

"You, Benny, you're like det painter. It took a lot of years and a lot of study, but you finally learned how to look at the same t'ings everybody else does, but you see de life lessons in everyday t'ings det other people don't. Don't sell yourself short, *boychik*. Det's a real talent. When you pluck an idea out of de air and wrap it up in a good story—and believe me, you know how to tell a story—and along wit' it you teach us sweet words from de Torah, you make us see everyt'ing a little different and det fills up de heart."

Uncle Joe was silent for a while as he forced himself to remain in one lane on the highway, but when they reached the outskirts of Youngstown and the streets were narrower, he swerved to the center of the road. Uncle Joe never trusted anyone to drive on either side of him.

"Benny," he said, ending the quiet. "You know, you wasn't always such a smart boy. When you was growin' up, you was one wild animal. I used to t'ink, 'dis kid got nuttin' but rocks in his head,' but look what happened. Somehow det Rabbi Academy turned dose coals into diamonds. I see dem shine from you every time you speak in de *shul*. What you got in your noggin is more valuable den all de buildings and all de paintings. De only trouble wit' you is you don't understand how important it is to make a decent dollah. You got dis funny idea det maybe people will respect you more if you don't t'ink about money and live like a bum, but you got it ass backwards. Dis is America. If you don't earn a decent dollah and live like a mensch, people won't respect you and dey won't listen to what you have to say. What's worse, dey'll t'ink our Torah is not worth respecting. Live like a *mensch*, Benny, you desoive it and so do we."

Mensch. That word rolled around Ben's brain as they passed Mercy Medical Clinic. He recalled the bitter antiseptic odor in the small single room where his father died seven years ago. That day was seared into his memory. His mother and his brother Art had gone out to talk to the surgeon but Ben remained, sitting on the hard wooden folding chair opposite the bed and read from a small Bible as his father slept. Sol's body was ravaged with cancer and tubes ran from every orifice to machines and plastic bags. Suddenly, he opened his eyes and saw Ben reading.

"Are you reciting Psalms?" he asked softly.

"No, Dad. Why would I do that?"

His father smiled bitterly. "Because that's what religious Jews do in the presence of someone who's dying, isn't it?"

"You're not dying, Dad. You're going to be fine," Ben lied. He told his father he had been reading the section of Genesis that deals with Jacob and Esau, the sons of Isaac.

"And what do you think about when you read that?" Sol's voice was weak but his eyes locked onto Ben.

"I think about me and Art," Ben said. "Art is so handy with mechanical things. He loves to fish and ski and do all that athletic stuff. I like to read."

His father smiled. Hesitatingly, he said. "So you think your brother Arthur is Esau, a savage, who would sell his birthright for a bowl of soup?"

Ben was painfully familiar with the text. It was hard not to identify with the gentler Jacob who pined for his father's favor.

Sol continued slowly. "And how do you explain why the saintly Jacob sold his hungry brother a bowl of soup? Why didn't he just give it to him?"

"Because he resented the fact that his brother Esau, whom everyone admired, was willing to exchange his birthright for a mess of pottage."

"Benny, Benny, don't make your brother out to be an Esau. Arthur's not a scholar like you, but he's a fine young man and believe me, he's no savage. And you, my dear son, you have so many wonderful qualities, but a saint you're not. Who says you should be? Just be a *mensch*. That's not easy, son, but if you succeed, I'll be very proud."

As BEN CLIMBED the brick steps with Uncle Joe to the porch of the narrow two-story wooden house where he grew up, Ben thought about his birthright—*be a mensch*. He had barely touched the handle of the old screen door before it flew open and his mother had her arms around him. His uncle looked on proudly while Bertha embraced him as though he were Elijah the prophet. "I can always trust Joe to bring you home safely. Come in, come in! I've made a little *nosh*, nothing to spoil your dinner." Bertha hooked his elbow and practically pulled him off his feet and into the house.

Inside the kitchen, Bertha had set Joe's cup of tea on the table with a crystal container of small sugar cubes and a huge plate of honey-covered nut cookies. "Please, boys, sit down and have a cup of tea. You must be famished." Uncle Joe made short work of the cookies.

"Benny, darling, you look so thin. Here, eat something." Bertha produced a glass of milk as though he were still her little boy, and a mound of mixed pastries—which Uncle Joe also finished.

After the milk and cookies, Ben went up to the bedroom he had shared with his brother. It felt claustrophobic. He didn't remember the room being so small. The picture of him and his brother on a pony wearing cowboy hats and pistols when they were three and five was still on the wall facing the bed. The dartboard still hung on the back of the door. He remembered the night when he and his brother had played darts instead of going to sleep. When their father opened the door to see what they were up to, a dart flew within a inch of his head.

Ben thought of the many nights he kept his brother up with questions like, "If God made us, who made God?" Even then Art had teased that he should become a rabbi and find out. He remembered the pillow fights and building castles in the sky. Memories filled every inch of that room, made thicker by the intoxicating smells of Bertha's holiday cooking. He could practically taste the cheesecake, blintzes and other dairy dishes she made traditionally for Shavuot. His mouth watered remembering her chicken soup with matzo balls, braised brisket, roasted chicken and all the tasty desserts as he lay on his old bed, his feet hanging over the edge of the mattress.

Perhaps the person who most appreciated Bertha's cooking outside the immediate family was Uncle Joe. It was really unfair how the relatives treated him. Was it because he was the only millionaire in the family or in spite of it?

Uncle Ziggy was especially cruel. "The man can't understand a word of Hebrew and he speaks Yiddish with that damned, barbaric *Galiztianer* accent." Ziggy insisted that Joe sit in the kitchen with the women at the weekly family get-togethers, while the men sat in the living room. Uncle Ziggy held the place of honor in the big red mohair chair. He was the owner of The Reliable Clothing Company on East Federal Street where he sold exclusively to the colored, but as he boasted, a better class of colored people. It was acknowledged that he was the one responsible for bringing Sol and his five sisters to America. It was never quite clear how Ziggy did it and there were rumors that he simply put their names on a list sent to HIAS, the Hebrew Immigrant Aid Society, but he always took exclusive credit for saving the family from the Czar, the Bolsheviks and later, Hitler. The family went along and gave Uncle Ziggy the place of honor at all family functions.

When Ziggy died, Sol insisted that Joe, his sister Thelma's husband, join the men in the living room. That was a precious gift and Joe never forgot it. After Sol died, Joe brought the family a kosher salami and a box of Tam-Tams every week. On the holidays, he would save a seat for his nephew in the synagogue so he could proudly sit next to Sol's boy who was studying for rabbi.

During his last trip home after Saturday morning services, the men who made up the prayer caucus assembled for a

Kiddush, which included several bottles of Seagram's Seven and Four Roses, plates of marinated herring and boiled potatoes, and *kichelach*—light and crusty egg cookies coated in sugar. All of the men in the group were old, but Old Man Kreutzer was the oldest. No one knew exactly how old he was and when Ben asked Uncle Joe, he said "plenty." He also explained that the secret of Kreutzer's longevity was the 10-ounce glass he brought with him to the Saturday morning Kiddush, which he filled to the brim with whiskey.

Ben's father had always liked Old Man Kreutzer, so he went over to wish him "Good Shabbos."

Kreutzer focused his one good eye on Ben. "Do I know you?"

"Yes, Mr. Kreutzer. I'm Ben Zelig."

He thought for a minute. "Doesn't ring a bell."

"Ben Zelig, Sol Zelig's son. You used to play pinochle with my father in the back of Gus's delicatessen."

"Sol Zelig . . . Sol Zelig. I don't know any . . . Wait a minute. Little Solly?"

Ben's father wasn't tall, but he towered over Old Man Kreutzer who was somewhere in the four-foot range. However, when Saul Rabinowitz, a six-footer, joined the game, Ben's dad became known as Little Solly.

"Little Solly—a real mensch. A fine chap," Kreutzer said, warming to the subject. "I loved your father. A swell fellow. Wait a minute, I remember now. Solly had two sons."

"That's right, Art and me."

"That's right, he had two sons. One of them died, which one are you?"

"I don't know where you heard that, Mr. Kreutzer, but both my brother Art and I are very much alive."

"Are you sure? I thought I heard . . . Maybe I'm thinking of somebody else. So you and your brother are Solly's boys. Oh yeah, I remember now. One flies around in airplanes."

"My brother Art is a captain in the Air Force," Ben said. "He's the pilot."

". . . and the other one . . ." old man Kreutzer's eyes were closed and he was thinking hard. Suddenly, his eyes opened wide. "The other one was studying for rabbi!"

"That would be me."

He looked at Ben, trying to focus his good eye. He looked and looked, then his face lit up as he touched Ben's cheek. "You're the one with the smiley face. I remember like it was yesterday. Maybe not yesterday, but I remember. Oh yeah, sure. Little Solly. I've never seen a man get so much pleasure from his boys, especially the one who was going for rabbi. A prouder man, there never was. You see, when we came to this country, everybody worked like a dog to make a living. Nobody had time to observe *Shabbos*, so we stopped going to temple. Then, we started to eat unkosher food, like the gentiles, because it was cheaper and little by little, we forgot what it was to be a Jew. It was depressing to think that nobody would ever study the holy books again. Being a Jew, living like we did for thousands of years, all that looked like it was vanishing forever. We used to say it was a cryin' shame that in our great America there's room for everything but *Yiddishkeit*. Our people lived through all kinds of expulsions and pogroms and everything else over the years, so you would think that when we finally came to America, the golden country where life is so good, we would return to our old ways. But we didn't."

He looked at Ben and smiled broadly. "So what happened in the end? Did everything that kept us together all those centuries die out?" He refilled his glass with whiskey to the brim and took a deep draught. He gargled involuntarily then swallowed. His eyes turned red, his voice got higher and his smile broadened.

"No, we're still here and you want to know why? I'll tell you why. Because a double miracle happened. Israel became a state and finally the Jewish people could defend themselves. Also, Little Solly's boy was going to become a rabbi and bring a whole generation back to the fold. Imagine that. How thrilled we all were. It gave us hope for the future. We won. Because of Israel and Solly's boy, we won. Everybody said the kid was so smart he coulda been a big doctor or maybe an important lawyer, but no, he went to become a rabbi and save Judaism." He took another gulp, a bigger one this time.

"You should only know what that meant to us. I'm not just talking about Solly, but all of us. The son—what's his name?"

"Ben. Ben Zelig."

"Of course, Zelig, like his father. Listen, if you ever run into that boy . . ."

BEN FELL INTO A DEEP SLEEP and when he awoke, he was ravenous. He could hear his mother calling him.

"Benny, do you think I made a perfect cheesecake so it could go uneaten? Come down here and say the *brucha*, so we can have dinner."

Ben threw some water on his face, smoothed his hair and went down to the kitchen. Bertha had set the table with her good dishes and heavenly smells greeted him.

"Not a single crack in my cheesecake and light as a feather. So smart of the rabbis to make a holiday where we have to eat cheesecake," Bertha said.

Ben said the blessings and then happily gave in as Bertha joyfully fed him all his favorite dishes. When he had his fill, he called New York. "I'd like to leave a message for Rabbi Joel Levin, the Rabbinical Placement Director. Please tell him Ben Zelig called. You can say I would like to . . ."

AFTER THE HOLIDAY, Ben returned to the Academy and found a message from Rabbi Levin. A congregation in Bridgeport, Connecticut had been looking for a full-time rabbi. In response to Ben's message, the placement director arranged for him to preach in the synagogue, the first Friday evening *Shabbat* service after ordination ceremonies. Ben would spend the rest of the weekend in Bridgeport, getting to know the movers and shakers. He would receive an honorarium of two hundred dollars plus round-trip train fare, a hotel room and meals for Friday through Sunday. If they liked one another, they would sign a contract.

Two weeks later, Ben was on the *bimah*, looking out at a congregation of three to four hundred well-dressed people in their middle years, plus some old timers, a smattering of teenagers and a couple of Roman collars from the neighboring churches. Ben had made a decision to move into his *mensch* phase and was determined to succeed.

For his sermon, Ben chose a controversial topic and decided to use the re-release of a popular film as the metaphor.

"One year ago, on April 15, 1969, the North Koreans shot down a Navy Lockheed EC-121 Reconnaissance plane over the Sea of Japan. President Nixon was furious and decided to attack North Korea with nuclear weapons. Although preparations were top secret, word got out and once again, the threat of nuclear war kept Americans up nights, watching their children sleep—and worrying. Fortunately, outcries from both parties rose to a crescendo that ultimately forced President Nixon to back down and nuclear weapons were off the table—for now.

"Realizing how close we had come once again to the brink of Mutually Assured Destruction, 20th Century Fox reissued *On the Beach,* a film that portrayed how a combination of arrogance, ignorance and simple mistakes could eradicate life as we know it on this planet. There was hardly a newspaper, TV or radio critic who didn't discuss the movie and how much more dangerous the world had become since the film was first released ten years ago."

Ben had a springboard.

"We can no longer deny the obvious," he told the congregation. 'We—all of us—are on the beach, waiting, wondering, when? How much longer can we dawdle while the world around us hovers on the brink of madness? Reason demands that we learn to live together on this increasingly crowded planet, but fear possesses us to compete with one another to acquire increasingly potent weapons. Resolving the incident in which an American reconnaissance plane was shot down over neutral territory was an important stopgap, but is there no way to permanently halt the ongoing race towards Armageddon?

Ben looked slowly around the packed synagogue. "We cannot undo the past, but we can learn from it. Come with me on a journey through time." With that, Ben took them on a brief tour of Jewish history. He reminded them that the reason Jews were able to endure millennia of unspeakable hardship and suffering was because they never lost faith in God's promise of a better tomorrow. "Yes, the world is badly damaged now, but our history has proven that we possess the power to repair it."

Ben led the congregation through allegories of the Bible, reminding them of their ongoing partnership with God that raises them above their beastly nature and of His covenants with Noah and Abraham that extend to every human being. Ben regaled them with inspiring lessons he had learned at the Academy and made sure to plant the seed of hope with the words of Theodore Herzl. "If you truly will it, it is not a dream." The sermon ended with the last image of the movie that had set the stage for his sermon: a banner that filled the entire screen with the words, "THERE IS STILL TIME . . . BROTHER."

Ben had submerged himself so completely in the imagery he had created that he wasn't sure he had finished until he heard himself say, "Amen."

The evening was—as Uncle Joe would say—a hit. The entire congregation lined up after the service to introduce themselves and thank the young rabbi for an inspiring evening. Ben knew that's what congregants said to every clergyman after every service, but this time they said it to him and although he probably should have taken it with a grain of salt, it felt good. The first family in line was the Grossmans. The husband, Morris, was a pudgy man with a Mickey Rooney complexion and fading red hair who talked out of the side of his mouth. Heather, the teen-age daughter had the misfortune to resemble her father and wore a plaid skirt, saddle shoes and a distant look in her eye. The wife, Charmaine, was a knockout. The tall, willowy brunette looked like she had been poured into her blue satin sheath. It was hard for Ben not to stare at Charmaine and she didn't make it any easier by staring at him. She shook Ben's hand warmly as her perfume wrapped around him in an intoxicating cloud.

Morris broke the spell. "I thought of becoming a rabbi once."

"Really?" Ben pretended to care.

"Yeah. My favorite story from the Bible was the one about Adam who was created out of earth, which is why men don't stink. But Eve was created out of Adam's rib and we know what happens to meat when it gets old." He barked out a laugh and nudged his wife. Charmaine didn't even try to feign a smile. Heather started to giggle, but stopped when her father continued.

"Remember that part, Rabbi?"

"I can't say I do," Ben said politely. "It's in the Bible, you say? Where exactly?"

"Who knows? It's been thirty years since I opened a Jewish book, but gems like that you don't forget. Look it up Rabbi, you'll find it."

For a brief moment, Ben wondered about the husband, but only for a brief moment. He watched Charmaine walk away and wondered if she had a sister.

All weekend congregants called him at his hotel to tell him how inspired they were by his message and hoped he would agree to become their rabbi. Many of them said they wanted to get to know him better.

"Would you honor us by coming to our house on Sunday, for a barbecue, some tennis and waterskiing on the lake?"

"You must be our guest at the club for the dinner dance on Saturday night."

Ben met some lovely people over the weekend, but couldn't get Charmaine out of his mind. What a beauty! She exuded femininity like no one he had ever met. That was what he would look for in a wife.

Late Sunday afternoon, Ben returned to his hotel dressed in shorts and a sweater. The Cohens, one of the wealthier families in the community, had invited him to play tennis at their private court. Al and his wife Lorrie were charming, intelligent people, not at all cynical like the beatniks Ben hung out with in Greenwich Village and definitely more fun to be with. *This is exactly where I should be at this stage of my life,* Ben thought.

When he entered the lobby, sweaty and tired, he saw Charmaine and her daughter standing at the front desk and his energy returned. "It's so nice to see you, Mrs. Grossman, and you, Heather. What brings you to the hotel?"

"Look, mom, the rabbi remembered our names. How do you do that? There must have been a thousand people in the temple on Friday night." Heather had an open, innocent face.

"The truth is, I don't remember everybody's name," Ben said. "Only those . . ." He caught himself. Where the hell was he going with this?

"Only those . . . ?" Charmaine had the most delicious smile, fortified by that intoxicating perfume. The answer was obvious, but Ben couldn't muster anything more than an embarrassed blush. Not attractive for a spiritual leader he realized and tried to smile through it.

"We were in the neighborhood and Heather thought it would be nice to stop in and say hello to the handsome young rabbi."

"Well, hello," Ben blushed even more. "Would you like to join me for a soft drink?"

"We'd love to," Charmaine said.

"I have to change," Ben said. "Al Cohen had me running all over the tennis court. Why don't we meet in the coffee shop in about fifteen minutes?"

Charmaine suddenly shifted gears. "I've got an engagement, but Heather can stay. Would that be all right?"

"I guess . . ."

"Heather, be on your best behavior. I'll be back around six, dear."

Ben watched as Charmaine sashayed through the revolving doors and out to the parking lot. Turning to Heather, he forced a smile. She smiled back.

"I'll just go upstairs and change," Ben said. "It'll only take a few minutes and . . ."

"I don't want to sit in the coffee shop all by myself. I'll come with you," Heather said.

"I don't think that's a good idea," Ben remembered that he had thrown his clothes over the furniture when he went out to play tennis. "My room is kind of messy."

"Believe me, I don't mind," Heather had made up her mind. "It's better than sitting here all by myself."

Ben ran his hand through his hair, perplexed. Then he started toward the bank of elevators. Heather followed. The ride up to the ninth floor in the mirrored elevator was awkward. They said nothing as Ben led her down the long, empty hallway past soiled food trays in front of closed doors. He was glad there was no one else around.

"Want something to read while I change?" Ben asked as they entered his room. Heather looked out the large window facing the parking lot then picked up the hotel guide and flopped into a chair. "Do your thing," she said.

Ben gathered the clothes he had strewn around the room earlier, took them into the bathroom and shut the door. When he came out a few minutes later, wearing a beige sport jacket, khakis and white bucks, he saw that Heather was lying on the bed, clad only in a pink bra and matching bikini panties. Her clothes were draped neatly over the chair.

Ben freaked, unable to utter a word. What the hell was going on? Ben's mind was a blank. Heather casually removed her bra, exposing full, round breasts. Ben didn't understand what was happening, but he knew that he would fall into a cauldron of lye if he didn't get her out of his room immediately. "Heather, what . . . uh . . . what are you doing?"

She simply smiled.

"Heather, how old are you?"

"Old enough."

"But you're under eighteen, aren't you?" Ben knew he would regret it if he let this go on much longer, but he'd never been in a bizarre situation like this. What was he supposed to say?

"I'm very mature, I assure you."

Little Heather wasn't so little anymore and that sent a shiver down Ben's spine. "Heather, you should not be doing this. Do you realize what could happen? You could get into serious trouble and so could I. What in the world makes you think that I, even if I were so inclined, and believe me, I am not . . ."

"You don't have to worry about anything," she said. "You don't even need a condom."

It took a moment for that to register. *I don't need a condom?* That could only mean—and it suddenly dawned on Ben. "Are you pregnant?"

"Only two months. Not a problem."

THE ONLY PERSON Ben could talk to about this was Uncle Joe, who he called as soon as he got Heather dressed and out of his room. "I couldn't believe what this girl told me! She's been promiscuous since she was twelve! Now she's seventeen and pregnant. Can you believe that?"

"What's not to believe? It's a goddamn minefield out dere. You gotta watch every step wit' dose bastids."

"What was she thinking, that I would have sex then agree to marry her and support her child? Did she think I was that naive?"

"Prob'ly. Dat's what people expect from rabbis."

"I don't believe that," Ben said defensively. "You should have seen the way I've been treated all weekend. I never got so much deference and respect in my life."

"Of course dey give you difference and respect. What does dat cost them? *Bupkes*. Dey smile nice, but down deep dey know rabbis are good in de book learning department, but pretty dumb everywhere else. So when dey got a problem and dey got to find a *schnook* to dump it on, you're a prime target. Enjoy de respect, Benny, it's nice but don't take it too serious. You did good getting de little *nafka* out of your room. You didn't touch her, did you?"

"I swear I didn't," Ben pleaded. "I've been debating whether to call her parents. I think they should be aware of what their daughter is up to."

"Benny, Benny. You're smart and you're smart, but in some ways, you're pretty dumb. Who'd ya t'ink put her up to dis whole t'ing?"

"Her parents?"

"Soitenly her mudda, from what you tell me. She sees dis young, wet-behind-de-ears rabbi and she t'inks to herself, dis guy is poifect. If a girl has a baby in seven months, it's a bastid, but if de father is a rabbi, it's a premie. Dis mother is no dumbbell."

"This is a small town. What do I do if I run into her?"

"You smile and say have a nice day. Believe me she won't be chasing you anymore. She tried to sell you damaged goods and you didn't buy, so why should she waste another minute on you? She's got to find another customer who's even dumber den you."

"That's so cynical, Uncle Joe."

"It's reality! How come dey don't teach you how to survive in de real world at dat rabbi academy? Don't dey tell you dat among all dose nice people who give you so much difference and respect dere are also a few sharks? You see, Benny, in the old country it was different. De good people looked out for dere rabbi so de bastids couldn't take advantage. In America, everybody looks out for demself and nobody even t'inks about protecting de rabbi. So, wit' nobody to look out for dem, American rabbis end up getting screwed more den anybody because dere so naïve. Dey like to t'ink people is basically good. Of course dey're wrong, but who wants to correct a rabbi? Dey'd radder give him all de respect he wants so dey can *kack* all over him if dey need to. In Europe, dey used to say a rabbi could walk wit' his head in de clouds because dere was always somebody to keep him from stepping in horseshit and soiling his trousers. It's different in America. Here, rabbis walk de same streets as everybody else and nobody gives a good goddamn, so you better watch where you're going, *boychik*, or your pants will get all *ferkakte*."

UNCLE JOE'S METAPHORS weren't the easiest to follow, but he understood the dark side of human nature better than most. Throughout Ben's student years, when he pondered moral imperatives, he thought Uncle Joe was an aberration. Where was Aristotle? Kant? They were certainly nowhere to be found in his universe of discourse. But now that Ben was venturing forth from the ivory tower, he could not deny that Uncle Joe's view of their species was in some ways more accurate than the nobler ones Ben had previously chosen to espouse.

Ben left Bridgeport on Monday. Despite what happened with the Grossmans the day before, he was exhilarated by all the approbation, the smiles, the warm handshakes and the promise of what lay ahead. But as the train entered Manhattan and passed through the graffiti and detritus of Harlem, Uncle Joe's admonition came back loud and strong. Ben was about to leave the sanctuary of the ivory tower. From now on, he would be walking the same streets as everybody else and he had better watch his step.

"They were very impressed," Rabbi Levin said when he called the following morning. "The Chairman of the Board of Directors of Temple Beth Israel called. They would like you to be their rabbi." He congratulated Ben and said all that remained was for him to go back for a meeting with the board and negotiate a contract.

Ben, negotiate a contract? How could he be expected to do that? In all his classes no one ever taught rabbinical students how to deal with practical issues—unless they occurred sometime before the twelfth century.

Who could he talk to? The only person who came to mind was Uncle Joe. "The going rate for newly ordained rabbis was fifty-thousand dollars a year," Ben told his uncle. "Everybody knows that, so what is there to negotiate?"

"Going rate, schmoing rate. Dey won't pay you a nickel more den dey have to so you better learn how to negosherate, *boychik*, or dey'll skin you alive."

A WEEK LATER, BEN ENTERED the ultra-modern conference room of Temple Beth Israel where he was introduced to six affable members of the Board of Directors. Uncle Joe assured him that he was ready. He had called Ben every night during the past week at exactly one minute past nine, after the long-distance rates dropped, and drilled him for an hour on the essentials of negosherating.

The five men and one woman on the board greeted Ben warmly when he arrived back in Bridgeport. They took pains to make the meeting appear cordial and not just a job interview. They offered him an elegant silk and leather upholstered chair while they sat in less elaborate, but comfortable, seats surrounding him.

"Not to worry!"

"Relax, Rabbi, we have a deal."

Wink, wink, elbow nudge.

"The only reason for the meeting is to work out a few details," one of the men said and proceeded to offer Ben coffee, a soft drink and anything else that would make him feel more at home and "part of the family."

That's exactly what Uncle Joe said they would do. How did he know?

Leonard David, known among trial lawyers as the Velvet Dragon, opened the discussion. Despite his casual slacks, cashmere sweater and brown loafers with tassels, his demeanor was solemn. "The important thing for us, Rabbi, is that we want to be fair."

Ben's first reaction was, why go on? Since they're going to be fair, did he really need to negotiate? But before he could open his mouth, the word "fair" rang a familiar bell in his head.

"Whenever dey tell you dey want to be fair or dey're being generous, you know dey're gettin' ready to cut off your *schmekel.*"

Leonard looked warmly at Ben as he continued. "Naturally, we wish we could be even more generous, but we're not a huge congregation and we don't have as much in our modest budget as we would like. Notwithstanding that unfortunate fact, we are prepared to offer you twenty-five thousand dollars for the first year." He smiled and raised his eyebrows for emphasis as though this were an unbelievably magnanimous gesture.

Ben was in shock. How could they offer him half of what the Rabbinical Academy Placement Director said was the going rate?

Ben saw Leonard's mouth move but all he heard was Uncle Joe's voice. "When a rich bastid cries poor, fold you legs quick before he shoves something up your ass." Here was Ben, like Daniel in the Lion's den, with nothing to protect him but his illiterate Uncle Joe's coaching. During their intensive rehearsals, Joe insisted that the most important part of negotiating is to keep your mouth shut. "Just smile and keep them guessing, *boychik*," he instructed.

So, when Leonard completed his remarks and looked to Ben for a fair response, Ben did exactly as he was prompted. He said nothing, but smiled back, first at Leonard, then slowly around the circle of all six members of the board. It was amazing how well that simple tactic worked. As the seconds ticked by and still, Ben said nothing; he realized the power of silence. When you say nothing, people think you really know something.

Howard Gewirtz broke first. "Let's not beat around the bush." He was chewing his unlit cigar faster and faster. "People who met you think the world of you. You know we want you to be our rabbi, so what's to talk about? Name a figure."

"Just make it fair, that's all we ask." Leonard wasn't about to give up control.

Saliva began to dribble down Howard's jaw. He was a stockbroker with a bleeding ulcer. He wasn't allowed to smoke but he couldn't kick the cigar habit, so the compromise was that he would chew unlit cigars until they got too slimy, then he would clip off the end with a small scissors and start again. Chew and clip, chew and clip into the large ashtray that rested on the arm of his upholstered chair. You could tell Howard was getting nervous, because he chewed faster and snipped more often. He started to cough and the dribble intensified.

"Howard, for God's sake." Mabel Soretsky, the only woman on the board, sat next to him wearing a lemon hat with a wide brim. She drew a small white tissue from her purse and tossed it onto Howard's lap.

He wiped his mouth, but continued to cough as he clutched his unlit cigar.

By the time all eyes came back to Ben, he was ready. Uncle Joe had drilled him on every detail of the plan of attack. It was up to him now to execute it. "De most important ting," he reminded Ben every night, "is de pants. Det's absolutely non-negosherate-able. If dey tell you dey can't afford, tell dem to shove de whole deal up der ass and det's all."

This being Ben's very first pulpit, he was totally ignorant of how rabbis are supposed to conduct contract negotiations. There were obviously other strategies he might have employed, but he would never have come this far had it not been for Uncle Joe, so Ben tried as best he could to strike a balance between Joe's instructions and the English language.

———

LEONARD EXPLODED. "You want fifty-five thousand dollars a year *plus* a pair of pants? This is Temple Beth Israel of Greater Bridgeport, for goodness sake. What do you think we are, a bunch of tailors?" All six members of the board appeared to share his indignation.

A month ago, that withering look alone would have been enough to make Ben capitulate but now all he heard was, "Whatever you ask for, dey're gonna hit de roof. So, let dem blow off steam. If dey really can't afford, which I don't believe for a second, dey'll shake your hand and ask you to go home and t'ink about it."

"Then what?"

"Den nuttin'. We'll look around to see if dere's someting better. If not, you can always go back and accept dere miserly offer, but I don't believe det's gonna happen. I heard enough rabbis speak to know dey ain't lettin you go so easy."

Ben looked at the curious faces sitting around him and waited, silently. They didn't end the meeting and they didn't ask him to go home and think about their offer. Leonard leaned towards him, his hands spread and his mouth open. He didn't look so intimidating anymore.

"I'm sorry gentlemen—and lady," Ben smiled at Mabel. "But that's what I require."

The atmosphere in the minimalist conference room suddenly became confused. The board members figured this would be a slam-dunk. Where does a novice rabbi get the *chutzpah* to haggle with Leonard David—or any of the other millionaires on the board for that matter? The thing that matters most is one's net worth, but how much is a rabbi worth?

They were stumped. Even Leonard didn't know the answer to that one.

"You've taken us completely by surprise, Rabbi, I can tell you that," Leonard sounded angry and disappointed. Ben felt terrible that he had upset the board members, but he had promised Uncle Joe that he would not deviate from the plan. Leonard looked puzzled. He waved his hands, but said nothing. He waited for a moment in agonizing silence, then, without looking at Ben, he said, "Give us a few minutes please, Rabbi."

"Of course." Ben walked to the door, butterflies doing pirouettes in his stomach. As soon as he got to the main floor of the synagogue, he immediately called Uncle Joe from the phone in the front office. "I'm afraid I screwed up. They're mad as hell."

"Whaddaya talkin'? In business, dere's no place for mad. You win or you lose. Dey're meeting wit you because dey want you should take de job. If dey get you, dey win. If dey don' get you, dey lose. But dey don't want to just win, dose bastids, dey want to win big. Det means dey got to get you for a little nothing. Don't worry about making dem angry. When you're negosherating you don't get angry. You pretend angry if it helps get the price you want and you stop pretending when it don't work."

"But maybe they don't have the kind of money I'm asking for in their budget."

"Dey don't have in dere budget? Rich bastids can always find money to put in a budget, but det's not de issue here. If dose bastids see dey can *schnorr* you down to a measly twenty-five thousand dollars, dey will have no respect for you and dey'll make from your life a misery. But if you stand up to dem, dey will respect you like crazy. Why? Because you kicked der ass and in business, de only thing dey respect is the person who kicked der ass."

"Would you please come back in, Rabbi?" Mabel was the one they sent. Back in the meeting room, Leonard looked at Ben with a half-chastising, half-sly look that he had obviously mastered over the years in the halls of the mighty. "Well, Rabbi, where do we go from here?"

Ben said nothing, but smiled back, as he was prepped.

"Is this some kind of ethical lesson you're teaching us through the allegory of a pair of pants?" Hoppy Halperin was the mattress magnate who greeted everyone with a big handshake and a warm smile, but now the smile was gone.

"Maybe not." Larry Owitz, the C.F.O. of Gimbel's department store, flashed his gold cufflinks and chimed in. "The rabbi says he wants a pair of pants. Okay, I think I understand where he's coming from. I know it sounds strange, but this kind of stuff goes on with the clergy. I got a call a couple of weeks ago from Bishop O'Shay. When my secretary told me who was on the phone, I forgot how you're supposed to talk to those people. What do you call a Bishop? I know the Pope is, uh, your majesty, but a bishop? Anyway, I said, 'Good morning your highness' and he seemed happy with that. I told him how honored I was by his call and everything. You know what he wanted? Two-hundred yards of red satin curtains for the new cathedral, what the hell's the name of it, on First Avenue?"

"Saint Mary's?" Hoppy really wanted to make a contribution to the conversation.

"I don't know," Larry Owitz said. "Anyway, that's when it hit me. Clergymen are strange about fabrics. Maybe that's why they're called Men of the Cloth. You know, material things, spiritual things. Could be, no?"

Morry, the stuttering C.P.A. shook his head. "Let's take. One step. Back." It was agonizing to watch him twist to form the words. "Beside the . . . pants. You named. A figure. That seemed awfully . . ."

"Fifty-five thousand dollars a year plus the pants," Ben reminded him.

Morry twitched. His stutter became worse. "You know, uh, your predecessor was, uh . . . More experienced. We, only paid him . . ."

"What kind of car did he drive?" Ben asked, paraphrasing Uncle Joe.

Morry twitched again. "What does that, uh, have to do with, uh, anything?"

"He drove an old Chevy, a dilapidated junker." Hoppy was back.

Howard snipped off another piece of the saliva-soaked cigar he had been chewing. "I can't tell you how embarrassed I was at the interfaith service at that new Catholic Church. You know, the one on Mohawk Drive with all the glass and steel? We had to call the AAA to tow the rabbi's car. My gentile neighbors wouldn't let up on me. 'You people are so rich,' he says to me. 'Why can't you buy your rabbi a decent car? Our priest drives a new Volvo.' I tell you I was never so humiliated. Listen, whatever we do, we got to insist the rabbi drives a nice car. What kind of car you got, Rabbi?"

"A rickety old Nash Rambler, but I'm in the market for a replacement." Ben looked at Howard, who smiled at him approvingly.

Leonard resumed control. "Now, Rabbi, let me get this straight. We're not talking about an entire wardrobe here, are we?"

"Just the pants." Ben looked around the conference room and realized that Uncle Joe, the ignoramus, had learned more about business from the School of Hard Knocks than any of these millionaires with degrees from top Ivy League colleges. They mastered economics; he understood human nature. Thanks to the scribbling on Uncle Joe's dashboard, Ben had also learned a few things

"What kind of pants, exactly?" Leonard was determined to get to the bottom of this.

"Well, that's the thing," Ben said. "Not just any pants, that's for sure. They've got to be 100 percent Italian wool, gray flannel, with reinforced knees, and you'll have to pay for alterations, of course. The cuff has to be above the shoe. I don't want my pants dragging in the street."

They looked at one another and finally at Raul Hollander, the only member of the board who wore a *yarmulke* and who, Ben later discovered, was the real power broker. As founder of Allied Radio, which later became Radio Shack, he was also the richest member of the Temple Board. Leonard and the others had gone as far as they could go. Until this moment, Hollander had not uttered a word. Now it was time for him to take over.

"Okay, Rabbi, what's the bottom line?" His raspy voice only added to his presumptive authority. The time for jockeying and allegories was over and everybody, including Ben, knew it.

Okay, Uncle Joe, here goes, Ben said to himself. "Gentlemen, and lady," Ben lowered his voice and spoke softly to make sure they had to pay attention to hear. "You are all immensely successful businessmen—and women—and you can negotiate the pants off anybody, pun intended, so in that regard I'm obviously no match for you, but I would like you to understand my position. Sure, I could live on less than fifty-five thousand dollars a year, but do you really want me to? If I can't afford decent furniture, should I keep my window shades drawn so the neighbors won't see how shabbily I'm forced to live? Do you really want me to spend my time scrounging for bargains in discount stores because I can't afford to buy a decent suit? Should I not have my lawn mowed because I don't have enough to pay the neighbor kid? Everyone in Bridgeport would have to conclude that the members of Temple Beth Israel don't feel that their rabbi deserves to live like a *mensch*. Is that how you feel?"

It was obvious from the way they looked at each other that Uncle Joe's point had hit the desired nerve.

"Okay, let's go back to negotiating," Ben said. "No matter how much I ask for, we all know you won't be happy unless I give up something, so let's wrap this up. Bottom line? The fifty-five thousand dollars is non-negotiable, but I am willing to give up the pants."

All eyes turned to Raul Hollander. He looked at Ben for a long moment, and then smiled and said, "You drive a hard bargain, Rabbi."

"But you got me to give up half of what of what I was asking for."

He walked over to Ben, took Ben's hand in his and turned to the others. "Congratulations, distinguished members of the board, we have ourselves a rabbi."

Everyone, with the single exception of Morry the C.P.A., stood up and applauded. Howard triumphantly mashed his slimy cigar butt in the ashtray. "No pants," he wagged a faux-threatening finger.

"No pants," Ben agreed.

"I got a condition for the rabbi," Howard continued. "I insist he become a member of the country club. I'll pick up his tab, but I want our gentile neighbors to see how we treat our rabbi." He turned to Ben "What do you say?

"You win," Ben conceded.

ON HIS NEXT TRIP to Youngstown, Uncle Joe beamed with pride as he drove Ben around to visit the relatives. He made him recite the story over and over again. After the first telling Uncle Joe knew every detail but he loved hearing it again and again.

"Do you think I got their respect?" Ben asked.

Joe smiled. "You did good, Benny. Dose bastids will t'ink different about rabbis from now on, I guarantee you."

"Should I have asked for more?"

Uncle Joe thought for a moment. "No, fifty-five t'ousand dollahs is a fair amount of respect your first time out." He reached over and pinched Ben's cheek. "Listen Benny, next year we'll negosherate again. And de year after det. You know you don't have to stay in det place, what de hell's de name, Bridgepark, all your life. Dere's bigger towns: Cleveland, Pittsboig. I even called my nephew in Chicageh yestiday. Big shul dere. Don't worry. I got it all figured out." Joe was positively triumphant.

Ben looked at the dusty dashboard of Uncle Joe's Eldorado and saw a wide swath of fresh scratches. He couldn't make out the figures but he knew Uncle Joe could.

eden

1979.

"SHE'S PRETTY, BEN, better looking than most of the girls you've dated, but a little young, don't you think?" Peter handed the snapshot of a smiling coed in a cap and gown back to Ben.

"Yes, she is good looking—and young," Ben said, "but curiously, the woman who answered the door didn't look anything like this photo."

Peter choked on his martini. "They pulled a switch on you?"

"Not exactly," Ben said, glancing at the snapshot. "It was the same girl, all right, only twenty-five years older. When her mother gave me the snapshot she did say it wasn't recent, but what she didn't tell me was that it was taken at her graduation from Vassar when I was in the second grade!"

It was two-thirty on a breezy spring afternoon. Ben and Peter Magnusson, vicar of The Good Sheppard Episcopal Church, were among the few diners left in the posh country club dining room. Three years ago Ben was installed as rabbi of Temple Beth Shalom in Acadia-on-Hudson. He met Peter at his first Clergy Association meeting and they became best friends almost immediately. On their weekly lunch dates, they left the sorrows and life-cycle crises of their respective congregants at the door. This was their time to let their clerical hair down and enjoy enlightened company. The conversation might begin with Wittgenstein's "Theory of Meaning," but it always found its way to Groucho Marx or George Carlin.

Peter thought the attempts at rabbinical matchmaking were comical and he started to laugh even before Ben got into the story of the matron from Vassar. He only stopped when the waitress interrupted to ask if they were ready to order. Peter had finished his second martini and Ben was still working on his first white wine spritzer.

"Have another," Ben offered.

"I should eat something first." Turning to the waitress, Peter said, "Bring me another Beefeater martini, but throw in a few olives this time."

She looked at Ben questioningly and pointed to his barely touched spritzer.

"The rabbi will have another popsicle," Peter said. He loved to taunt Ben about his inability to drink. Ben couldn't understand how anyone could drink more than one martini at lunch and not fall on his face. If Ben drank more than one glass of wine, he would spend the rest of the day walking up a steep hill. Amazingly, the more Peter drank, the more cogent he became. "Make that a tuna fish sandwich on wheat toast for me," Ben said, "and in addition to the olives, Father Magnussen will have . . . ?"

The waitress tapped her pencil impatiently on her pad as Peter studied the menu. Ben ordered for him. "The vicar will have the rib-eye steak," he said, "and a large Caesar salad, double order of French fries, assorted grilled vegetables and chocolate cake for desert. What he doesn't finish, he will take home." Ben's congregants never allowed either of their revered guests to pick up a tab, but they made sure the vicar's parishioners—who knew full well that he was raising a family of four children on his meager salary—received a full report.

"So what has this Vassar graduate been doing since you were in the second grade?" Peter asked, looking at the photo again.

"Not much. Her mother said she's considering several careers but so far hasn't figured out what she wants to do with her life. Fortunately, there's no pressure because daddy set up a substantial trust fund so she can explore as long as she likes. I don't know if the mother told me that to throw me off about the age thing or to let me know 'daddy' is well-heeled."

"Since when are you interested in P.H.G.s?"

Ben wondered where Peter learned the expression P.H.G. and couldn't help smiling. His Uncle Joe, the only member of Ben's family who was illiterate and a millionaire and Ben's source for all things that needed *negosheratin'*, liked to say, "it's just as easy to fall in love with a rich girl as a poor one, so keep an eye out for P.H.G.s." That is, *poppa hut gelt* (father with cash).

"P.H.G.? Peter, you know me better than that! What I'm hoping to find is someone I can share my life with. I hate living alone," Ben said. "That is the sad, awful truth. It's also true that as the rabbi of a close-knit community, I live in a fish bowl and every move I make becomes the latest gossip. I've gone on a few blind dates, but every one of them was disastrous. I know what I'm looking for—but where do I find her?"

Peter looked at the photo of the girl in cap and gown. "How did you find this one?"

"I didn't. Her relatives found me. After a meeting of my book club last week, Harriet Schreiber asked if she could have a word with me. 'You outdid yourself today, Rabbi,' was the butter-up. 'Your review of that book, *To Jerusalem and Back*, was brilliant. I was so impressed I promise to buy the book and read it and I'm not saying that to be nice. Ask anyone. With me, what's in the heart is on the tongue.' Then she gave me this look. 'Forgive me if I'm crossing a line here, but it pains me that a man so intelligent—so handsome—lives alone.' How the hell was I supposed to respond to that?" Ben asked.

"What *did* you say?"

"Nothing. Before I could come up anything, she hit me again. 'After a hard day in the *shul*, wouldn't it be nice to come home to a loving wife and maybe, with God's help, a family?'

"She stared at me but I still couldn't think of anything to say so she dove right in. 'I apologize if I'm being too forward, but if I don't share this with you, I'll burst.' She opened her purse and pulled out the picture. 'This is the girl for you, Rabbi. Look at her. Is she not beautiful? And it's not just looks. Seville is her name and she's smart, she's funny, speaks French and what a dancer! Okay, she's my daughter but that's beside the point. When I first met you, I knew. I said to myself, I said, what a perfect match! And everyone I talked to agrees. The rabbi and Seville? Couple number one!'

"Before I could say anything, the grandmother jumped in. The old lady grabbed my lapel and stared at me with her one good eye. 'She's really good at the sex stuff!'"

Peter went into a coughing jag and raised his hand for Ben to stop. Ben paused while the vicar drained his martini glass.

"I felt like Gulliver trapped by raging Lilliputians," Ben continued. "There was no way to put them off. They insisted I call the girl then and there, and . . ."

The waitress delivered the drinks and all the food, which Peter proceeded to arrange so that it could easily be put into doggy bags.

"*Nu?*" Peter smiled. Ben couldn't get over the vicar's ease with Yiddishisms. "*Nu,* so what happened?"

"I caved," Ben conceded. "Two days later, I was in a gilded glass elevator on Sutton Place South moving rapidly toward the forty-second floor when I suddenly got that uneasy feeling in my gut. How did I let them nab me again? Over the past three years, I had gotten myself fixed up with a dozen or so blind dates and every one of them turned out to be a disaster."

"What made you think this was going to be any different?" Peter sucked the gin out of the olive then put it back in his glass.

"One of the reasons I buckled was that a cousin of hers is a particularly striking woman and the wife of a rabbi-turned-lawyer who always sat in the first row of my lectures. She was bright, funny and managed to distract me regularly by crossing and uncrossing her long legs to the point where I fantasized that the cousin they were trying to pawn off on me just might be something like her. Obviously, I was wrong. When this girl—this woman—opened the door and said, 'Hi, I'm Seville. Are you Ben?' I froze."

"What did you do?"

"For what seemed like forever, I just stood there. She bore a faint resemblance to the cute girl in the cap and gown but she was older—much older. In fact, she resembled the grandmother more than her mother. And I think it was mutual. From the disappointed look on her face, it was clear that she had expected a much more mature man. I guess the title rabbi implies graying temples and a white beard. It was so awkward. Obviously, we had both been played for suckers and neither of us knew what to do. I had to find a way to get us out of that car wreck as quickly as possible so I said the first thing that flew into my head.

"'Is this apartment 3902?' I asked.

"'No, this is 4202.'

"'Sorry,' I said and pretended to feel foolish. She slammed the door and I made a dash for the elevator."

Peter laughed so hard, his martini dribbled down his jaw. "You're going straight to hell, you know that."

"It was humiliating for both of us, but I couldn't think of anything else at the moment."

"What happened after you left? Did you call the woman?"

"Of course. I waited about half an hour, and then phoned to say that I received an emergency call from the synagogue and had to rush back to Acadia. I apologized for standing her up and told her I'd try again sometime. I called her mother and made a similar excuse just to cover my ass."

"Did they buy it?"

"I have no idea."

"Why do you continue to accept blind dates from your parishioners? You know it's a disaster waiting to happen."

"I can't help it. I'm so frigging lonely and they're so aggressive! You should hear them.

'Please explain it to me, Rabbi. What do you have to lose by going on a date with the perfect girl?' Everybody's got the perfect girl, it seems—until I meet them and discover that it's just another catastrophe in the making."

Peter suddenly became uncharacteristically silent.

"What's up?" Ben asked.

"Nothing."

"I repeat the question."

"I can't help it, Ben." Peter started to slice his steak, but it was clear he was saving the best part for his doggy bag. "When you talked about the perfect girl, someone actually came to mind."

"Oh no! Not you, too."

"That's why I won't say another word."

"Who is she?"

"Forget it, Ben. I wasn't thinking."

"Come on, Peter. What's she like, this perfect girl?"

"I really don't want to talk about it."

"Why? Is she not beautiful, is she not brilliant, is her father not a multi-millionaire, and is she not perfect for me?"

Peter put down his knife and fork. "Yes and no. She is beautiful, smart, spiritual and extremely talented. Her father *is* very wealthy, but he's disowned her so there won't be any of that coming her way. I must say she is perfect for someone, but not you, okay?"

Ben was hooked. Peter's wife, Bridget, was an unusually attractive, intelligent woman and Ben respected his taste.

"Why is she not perfect for me?"

"For one thing, she's not Jewish."

AS HE DROVE ACROSS the Triborough Bridge toward Broadway and 41st Street to meet Peter's idea of "the perfect girl," Ben tried to visualize what she would be like, this renegade daughter of one of the richest families in Acadia who dropped out of Radcliffe College in defiance of her parents and took a job first as bartender, then joined an improvisational theatre group and eventually became a hugely successful Broadway actress. Ben had not dated a girl who wasn't Jewish since high school, but Peter's description hit every one of his buttons. The fact that she was also interested in philosophy and Peter had lent her his copy of "The Varieties of Religious Experience" by William James definitely rendered her kosher in Ben's lonely mind. Peter had mentioned something about a health issue but didn't know any details so Ben didn't give it much thought.

This was Ben's first experience meeting a Broadway star backstage and he was determined to impress. He felt particularly chic in his new double-breasted cashmere coat as he walked from the parking lot on Tenth Avenue towards the Majestic Theater. On the corner of Eighth Avenue, a wino wrapped in a combination of cardboard and rags winked at Ben and pointed to his coat.

"Whooee, check out our bad vines," he grinned. "We're looking good tonight!" his new friend declared as he walked alongside Ben, waving to passers-by, smiling broadly and pointing to *their* coat. Ben pretended not to notice, but he was enjoying it and it was hard to restrain his grin.

Somewhere in the crowd, Ben lost his escort. At first he was relieved, but there was no denying that he had enjoyed the attention. Ben joined the long line at the box office behind an affectionate young couple with well-scrubbed Midwestern looks; honeymooners he guessed.

Fortunately the line moved rapidly and when Ben got to the will-call window and gave his name, the woman smiled at him. "I see you have a house seat," she said.

"Is that good?" he asked.

"The best," she said. "You're going to love it."

When the usher directed him to a seat in the third row, center aisle, Ben understood. This was where they sat the celebrities. He couldn't help looking around to see if there were any nearby.

THE SHOW WAS *Fiddler on the Roof* and MaryAnne played Tzeitel, Tevya's eldest daughter. The *babushka* she wore, which was pulled slightly back, made her appear so vulnerable. She was even more beautiful than her picture. Her movements were lyrical and when she sang, her voice was rapturous. Ben was so absorbed in the drama that when she cried, "Papa, please don't make me marry Lazar Wolf, the butcher," Ben was genuinely upset. Later, in the marriage scene, when she stood under the *chupah* with her beloved Motel the tailor, her face was glowing. So was Ben's.

When the curtain went down, Ben leapt to his feet and applauded with all his might. A couple in the row behind him asked him to sit down. Sit down? After what he just experienced? That would be sacrilege.

Backstage, Ben followed the stagehand's instructions and went up the flight of stairs to a door that read, "MaryAnne Pembroke." There was a star on the center of the door.

When it opened, Ben thought he was looking at a fantasy. She wore a medium-length Japanese embroidered silk gown and her freshly scrubbed face glowed. He wanted to tell her how brilliant she was, how beautiful. Nothing came out. Shyly, he squeaked out, "I'm Ben."

"I guessed." She forced a distracted smile. Her long black hair was the perfect frame for her aristocratic face. She had a small straight nose, sensitive lips and piercing dark brown eyes.

Ben noticed she was holding a telephone receiver. "Yes,

of course, I'm still here . . ." she said, lifting it to her ear. She waved Ben in with her free hand and pointed to a chair. Her attention was clearly on whomever she was talking to, so he continued to stand. "Call me back as soon as you know," she said. "It doesn't matter. Anytime. Thanks, Alan."

She looked distraught as she hung up the phone and Ben suddenly felt like he was intruding. He waited for a long, silent moment, not knowing what to do or say. Then she turned to him and smiled warmly, although her eyes showed signs of lingering anxiety. "Hi Ben, I'm MaryAnne. How did you like the show?"

"How did I *like* the show? One of the great experiences of my life!" Ben couldn't restrain his enthusiasm. "You were so . . ."

The door flew open and a cute girl, about MaryAnne's size and shape, but with a head full of sable curls, huge hazel eyes and brilliant teeth, popped in.

"Please don't leave the show," she pleaded. "We need you. I need you." MaryAnne embraced the visitor.

"You'll be great, Marci. I have no doubt about that."

Marci noticed Ben. "You look like some kind of power dude. Are you her agent? Would you please convince her to stay? The show will collapse without her."

"This is Ben, Marci. He's not an agent, he's a rabbi."

She looked him up and down. "Aren't you kind of cute to be a rabbi?" she teased as she ran her hand down Ben's tie.

"Marci, you're gay," MaryAnne gently reminded her.

"Not always," she said, but judging from her immediate loss of interest in Ben, he assumed she was always. She gave MaryAnne a big hug. "I can't believe you're leaving the show. Come see me and promise you'll give me notes."

"Promise," MaryAnne pledged.

When Marci left, the room became suddenly quiet.

"You're leaving the show?" Ben couldn't hide his dismay. He didn't want to pry but felt he had to say something. "You were magnificent! You were . . . Are you just tired of it or are there bigger plans in the making?"

She thought for a moment. "It's time to move on."

The telephone on her dressing table rang. MaryAnn picked it up immediately. "What's the story?" Her face screwed up as she listened. "Shit. Of course . . . Whatever you can do . . ."

Ben was obviously intruding so he gesticulated: "I'll meet you outside."

MaryAnne was oblivious as he slipped out the door. Ben wasn't sure why he felt so disappointed that she was leaving the show. She was so perfect! It was a mild evening and Ben exited the stage door with his cashmere coat draped over his shoulders. Suddenly, he found himself surrounded by a screaming mob begging him to sign their programs. Ben tried to tell them that he wasn't in the show but they were so busy jostling and shoving one another for autographs, they didn't listen, so he picked up one of the programs and signed his name. A young girl looked at it and her face screwed up. "Ben Zelig?" She shouted above the noise of the throng. "You're nobody!"

NOBODY?! Ben was mulling that over an hour later as he sat in a dark oyster bar called Triton's Tomb. The walls were covered with large trawling nets and thick ropes hung from the vaulted ceiling. Despite the ornate Greek urns on stands around the room and the looming statue of Triton holding a trident at the entrance, the restaurant was gloomier than it was classical.

The table where MaryAnne and Ben were seated shook every time he leaned on it, but that didn't seem to bother MaryAnne. She was lost somewhere inside her head, slowly stirring her cloudy white ouzo cocktail with a striped cocktail straw. He wanted so badly to reach her, to tell her how deeply her performance had moved him, that she was so talented. What he really wanted was to talk to her, but he didn't know how to open that door. Ben watched her swish a trail through her drink for endless minutes. Finally, he said, "Would you like me to get some duckies to float in your ouzo?" He expected her to laugh or at least, smile.

"I'm sorry, Ben," she said from a distance, "But . . ."

The waiter appeared at her elbow with a telephone on a tray. "Miss, there is a call for you." He plugged the phone into the wall, set the base on the table and handed her the receiver.

"Thank you," MaryAnne said. The waiter discreetly departed.

"Hello?" She adjusted the receiver to her ear. "Uh-huh . . ." She got up quickly and started to pace nervously behind their table, holding her phone with one hand and the receiver in the other.

Ben looked at the oysters she ordered but hadn't touched. Ben had never eaten shellfish and from the looks of those raw, slimy things floating in stony shells, he couldn't imagine why anyone would want to. The tuna sandwich on white bread in front of him was swathed in mayonnaise and didn't look at all appetizing either. Nor was the tepid cider in a heavy mug with a stick of cinnamon floating in the center. It seemed like a cool thing to order, but it was hard to believe apple juice could taste so cloying. Ben heard a crash and saw that the phone cord had knocked MaryAnne's drink onto the floor. His instinct was to get up and see if she was all right, but she was so involved in her phone call that she walked past the broken glass, not noticing. Ben decided not to interfere and instead signaled to the waiter.

When she returned, MaryAnne flopped down in the wooden chair opposite Ben and practically slammed the phone back on the table. She sat silently, absorbed in her thoughts. Then, noticing the new ouzo cocktail Ben had ordered to replace the one she dropped, she leaned over and gave him such a big hug he had to hold onto the shaky table to keep it from turning over. When she sat back down, Ben saw that her eyes were moist.

"Bad news?"

She clenched her jaw, holding back tears. Then, she shrugged and took a sip. After a longs silence, she said, "Talk to me, Rabbi."

"About . . . ?" Ben didn't know if she was referring to life in Acadia, their mutual friend, Peter, movies, the theater or if she was just trying to find a subject that was less distressing than the one that came out of the phone.

"Life, death, good, evil, love, cruelty, why we're on this planet. Tell me everything you know." She took a yellow pad out of her bag and set it on the table.

Ben was surprised that she was actually going to take notes. There was genuine passion in her voice, but he wasn't sure what she was asking. "What I know about—*all that*? To be perfectly honest, not much."

"But you've studied the holy texts. You must have spent years in the company of saintly men . . ."

"And women," Ben thought that might provide an opportunity to move away from these arcane subjects.

"So you must know a lot," she rummaged urgently through her purse and came up with a vial of pills. She took one and swallowed it with a sip of the ouzo, then turned to Ben.

"So?" She clicked her pen, ready to write.

"MaryAnne, all I have are my own beliefs. I can't say that they are any truer or more valid than anyone else's. I can't prove anything if that's what you're asking."

"I am not asking for proof. I want you to tell me what you *know*."

"That could take a long time."

"That was my oncologist on the phone, Ben. I may not have a long time."

HOURS PASSED as she questioned Ben about theology, eschatology and mysticism, writing down voluminous notes in the yellow pad that was already bulging with diagrams, sketches, assorted articles and ads for alternative cures affixed by cellophane tape.

He kept trying to work the conversation back to what the oncologist had said on the phone. Finally, he just came right out and asked. "What's the prognosis?"

"It's nothing I can't deal with, so don't you worry about it," she said, and then took another sip of her drink. Fortified, she swished her fourth oyster around in some cocktail sauce and God knows what else. Ben had never seen anyone eat so slowly. His dull tuna sandwich, which couldn't have been any worse than her slippery little barnacles, was long gone.

Somehow, despite the exhilaration of meeting this stunningly gifted woman, all Ben could think about were hints of her lurking disease. In the nine years Ben had been a rabbi, first in Bridgeport, then Lake LaSalle, and now Acadia, he witnessed more sickness and death than most people do in a lifetime and he never learned how to cope with it. Every time he held the hand of someone with a terminal condition it was a deeply emotional experience for him. Ben discovered early on that the best way to help was to listen, not talk, but MaryAnne kept drilling him for answers to the unanswerable. She never brought up her illness, much less her fears or hopes or dreams. Ben was distressed that he had nothing to give her.

She studied his face. "Don't be so glum, Rabbi, you're not the one who's dying."

"Sure I am, MaryAnne," Ben responded gently. "We all are. Life *is* terminal, you know."

She thought about that and then wrote something in the ever-decreasing margin of her yellow pad. Something in her notes caught her eye and she transfixed Ben with her intense gaze.

"The Old Testament," she said bluntly. "What kind of weasel was Abraham? According to the story in Genesis, he told that petty Egyptian warlord that his wife Sarah was his sister. He must have known that scumbag would hit on her. How could God forgive him so easily for that kind of cowardly behavior?"

"What makes you think Abraham was forgiven?"

"Didn't God bless him and reward him with an unusually long life? Read your Bible, Rabbi."

"I have, and from everything I've studied—and experienced—I can tell you that a long life is not necessarily a reward *or* a blessing." He was about to elaborate when she put up her hand to stop him while she scribbled.

When she finished writing, she looked at Ben and smiled for the first time. "I like smart men. Go on."

"I'd better stop here," Ben said, trying to lighten the conversation. "I may become stupid and you'll hate me."

"What I hate are cowards," MaryAnne said and grabbed Ben's hand. It excited him and, under the circumstances, he wasn't sure how appropriate that was. "Take your best shot, Ben. Tell me why living isn't always better than the alternative."

"It usually is, but not always. There are times when every minute is excruciatingly painful, not only physically, but also emotionally and spiritually. I've witnessed that and, believe me, it's no blessing. The important point, if you accept the fact that life is terminal, it is not the length of the journey, but whether you're on the right path. The truly significant thing . . ."

"Stop!" MaryAnne help up her other hand. "You're slipping into a sermon and I hate sermons. Get back to Abraham. He got far more than he deserved considering all the times he screwed up. You have to agree with me about that." She lifted her glass, but it was empty. Ben motioned to the waiter that she was ready for a refill.

"No, I don't agree," Ben said. "Nobody gets a pass in the Old Testament. When someone messes up, whether they're patriarchs, prophets or kings, there's a price to pay. Sure, Abraham faltered more than once and made some stupid mistakes, all of which are clearly delineated in the Old Testament and not glossed over, by the way, but he took a lot of hits, too. Think of his soul-wrenching anguish over Isaac. What goes on in a father's heart when the path he's chosen risks the very life of his child?"

"Strange archetypes you Jews have. The best of them do some awfully reprehensible things."

"The question is—what can you learn from the choices they made?"

MaryAnne thought about that as the waiter set the ouzo cocktail in front of her. Stirring it with her straw, she pondered.

"You've got a point there. I'll take the fiery Old Testament Jews any day over the sanctimonious cherubs of the New Testament who look like they're either faking orgasms or doing disgusting things to other sanctimonious cherubs." Ben couldn't hold back a chuckle.

"If you want to understand the Old Testament," he said, trying his best not to sound pedantic, "think of charts that show the physical evolution of our species from tree swingers to Homo Erectus. The Bible chronicles our moral evolution by placing people, real or mythical, in situations everyone can understand. By exposing their weaknesses . . ."

"Got it, don't get rabbinic on me. No sermons!" She said, scribbling the words into an empty space at the bottom of a page. MaryAnne had no patience for anything that sounded glib. She was looking for something deeper, something solid from which she could draw strength.

"I don't want to hear allegories," she said. "I got all I can handle from the Catholics and the yogis." She stopped for a moment and took a long sip. "I thought of becoming Catholic once, did I tell you that?"

"No, you didn't." Ben wistfully hoped she would express some interest in him beyond religion and philosophy. He watched MaryAnne take a long sip and slowly cruise through her notes. Despite her eagerness to find answers, her questions were beginning to blur.

"Where did it all happen, Ben? What was it like? Ur of Chaldees? What did it feel like to be there in Abraham's time? Is Jerusalem as magical a place as they say it is? I hear that on the Sabbath you can see reflections of the Divine in the eyes of the devout. Should I go there?"

"I have an idea," Ben said. He leaned toward her. "Why don't we go to Jerusalem together?"

MaryAnne smiled and brightened up for a brief moment, then became very quiet. "Ben," she said after a long silence, "where is Eden? Was there really a healing garden called Eden?"

"I have no first-hand knowledge, but I can tell you what the *Kabbalah* says. It may sound like a sermon, but it isn't."

"Okay," she smiled.

"The sages believe there actually was a place called Eden. It was, they say, a paradise unlike any other. Lush fragrant flowers, colorful plants and an endless variety of trees flourished in every direction as far as the eye could see, but its most dazzling feature was the sparkling river that ran through its heart."

"Where is that river, Ben? How can I find it?"

"Believers say it will find you. That river, they contend, continues to flow through the souls of The Just in every generation."

"The Just? Like in Andre Schwartz Bart's book, *The Last of the Just*? Is that from the *Kabbalah*? Tell me about them, Ben. I need to know how to become one of The Just."

Everything she said tugged at Ben's heart. He was profoundly affected by her and wanted so much to help, but how? Her anxiety was so intense she didn't notice that she was totally engulfed in a world of allegory. She needed some idea, some vision, some hope, something strong enough to support her now and what it was made of didn't matter.

Suddenly, MaryAnne winced, doubled over and reached into her purse. She seemed to be having a stomach spasm. A small bottle fell on the floor. Ben picked it up. The label read *M.S. Contin*—an extract of morphine. He handed the small bottle to MaryAnne and she quickly downed a pill with a sip from Ben's untouched water. She sat quietly for several minutes, dealing with the throbbing tremors rippling through her body. When the pain passed, she picked up her notes, looked at them and turned to Ben, confused.

"What was I talking about?"

"Eden," Ben said. It was painful to look at this magnificent woman whose skin was smooth and vibrant, knowing that underneath the surface was a gnawing malignancy.

"Of course, the thirty-six righteous souls in every generation! They . . . They what? What did they do, again?"

Ben talked about the legend of the *lamed vavniks*, thirty-six anonymous saintly people whom no one recognizes but whose deeds convince God to save their entire generation from extinction.

MaryAnne tried to scribble fast as Ben talked. She had obviously chosen to believe that some combination of notes, insights and formulae might provide the information she needed to cure herself. It was agonizing to watch her fight so hard through what must have been a heavy medicated fog descending from her head to her heart as she searched for that elusive answer. Ben tried every way he knew to comfort her, but what could he say? MaryAnne was getting groggy and the more her consciousness drifted, the more anxious she became about finding the answer she believed was somewhere in her notes. She went through them again, page after page until she dropped the pad on the table in despair and looked at Ben. "What exactly did they have to do, those thirty-six people, to convince God not to let us die?"

It was after two when the menacing bouncer of Triton's Tomb hulked over them and pointed to the door. "Out!"

MaryAnne refused to leave. Ben had never been thrown out of anyplace before and it would have been a harrowing experience for him if she hadn't been there.

"Look lady," the giant said. "We closed over an hour ago and we've asked nicely several times and you haven't budged. So I'm telling you—get your ass out of here before I pick you up and throw you out."

"How long do you have to live?" she countered defiantly.

"What!"

"I know the answer. You've already lived too damn long." She turned to Ben. "Explain this to me, Rabbi. Why do Neanderthals like him get to live so long while the good die young? I demand a reasoned theological response, not some allegory. This worm is probably one of the thirty-six vermin who give us humans a bad name. Can't God see that?"

Ben managed to get her to his car. When they arrived at MaryAnne's, she could barely walk straight. He practically carried her up to her apartment. When she finally figured out how to unlock her door, she asked Ben if he would stay with her. Maybe he should have thought more about what that might entail, but it was late, he was tired and she needed him.

Half asleep, MaryAnne came out of the bathroom in a modest white granny nightgown and collapsed onto Ben, who was fully dressed and stretched out on her modest double bed. Her yellow pad lay next to him as she passed out on his chest. Ben allowed himself to believe he was somehow protecting her. The serene look on her face was the same as when she stood next to Motel the tailor under the *chupah* in the play, just a few hours ago. The comfort he felt with her head on his heart enabled him to drift off peacefully.

A few hours later, with her eyes still shut, she said. "Tell me about *The Last of the Just.*"

"You said you read Andre Schwartz-Bart's book."

"Yeah, but I don't get it. There are supposed to be thirty-six righteous people in every generation, scattered around the world, right? And their miraculous deeds prevent God from completely destroying life on earth, right?"

"So the legend goes," Ben agreed.

"But in the book, this guy manages to get himself *into* Auschwitz, where he will most assuredly be gassed, so he can spend his dying moments with the woman he loved. What's miraculous about that? Is that the most significant deed one can perform on earth?"

"Solomon tells us the only thing that can conquer death is love."

She opened her eyes and looked up at Ben. "Do you believe that?"

"Does it really matter what I believe?"

She rolled back and cradled her head in the crook of his arm. "It's beginning to matter to me," she said softly. Semi-awake, MaryAnne had the sweet smell of sleep in her hair and Ben dared not think about what was to come. The only thing he knew for sure was that every breath she took now was divine and he prayed for it to continue.

THE SUN WAS COMING UP as Ben reached the Cross Bronx Expressway. Cool air flowed through the car bringing with it the scent of freshly cut grass. What a night! MaryAnne was the most intriguing woman he had ever met. Just lying next to her, fully clothed, filled him with a sense of ease and contentment—but he couldn't stop thinking about the looming threat of that malevolent disease and wondered what he could do to help her.

Ben arrived at the synagogue around seven-thirty when Hank Sperling and the other nine old men were coming out of the small chapel next to his study. "What's the matter, Rabbi, you too good for the Hank Sperling Religious Committee Prayer Service? One day a month! Is that so hard for you to remember?"

What could Ben say? Prayer that comes from the heart is a cornerstone of his life, but mechanical recitation of rote words is worse than meaningless, it's a hollow mockery. It's sex without love or reverence. Ben knew what was truly divine, what aroused his passion, what was spiritual and transcendent. It was MaryAnne, asleep in his arms, temporarily free of pain and the terrors of her disease.

"I was detained," Ben said and walked into his office.

In his study, surrounded by books lining the shelves and lying open on the vast expanse of his desk studded with marked passages and notes, the only thing Ben could focus on was MaryAnne. Was it too early to call? Was she feeling any better? Did she want to talk to him, see him? He longed for her, to be with her, hold her, sleep alongside her, inhale her sweet fragrance and hopefully, help her find some solace. Over the years, Ben had a variety of sexual experiences but nothing ever meant as much to him as the few chaste hours he spent with MaryAnne lying in his arms.

Ben devoted the better part of the morning to clearing his desk, answering calls and working on an article for the Temple Weekly. He remembered MaryAnne's interest in the legend of the thirty-six righteous and he made a point of reviewing relevant sections of the *Zohar*, the core text of the *Kabbalah*, so he would have a pretext to call.

Thoroughly armed, he picked up the phone. After three rings, her voice came on. It was strong, mellifluous and direct. "This is MaryAnne. You may leave an inspirational message or hang up now. Name and phone number optional." Ben put the phone down immediately. Inspirational message? Even the *Kabbalah* might not pass that test.

For the rest of the day, Ben met with congregants and reviewed the Hebrew School curriculum with the teaching staff, but he couldn't get MaryAnne out of his head. *Should I have said something before hanging up?* he wondered. *What passes for an inspirational message?* He would never have the *chutzpah* to think anything he had to say would qualify as inspirational.

In the late afternoon Ben had one of his most ineffective counseling sessions of his career with a feuding couple who addressed each other in the third person, and their twelve-year-old son. The boy never looked up from his comic book as his parents raged on. Ben heard nothing but MaryAnne's voice in his head. As soon as his congregants left, he called again and got the same message. This time Ben wasn't going to hang up.

"MaryAnne, dear lovely lady," he said. "This is Ben, as in last night. You've been on my mind all day but I haven't left a message because . . ."

"Hi, Ben," her cheery voice broke in.

"MaryAnne! I . . . Are you all right?"

"Yeah."

Ben wasn't sure how to continue. "Last night you were in such distress, I didn't know what to think."

"I have good days and bad ones. Last night was one of the worst. Today the sun is shining and I feel wonderful except for a slight hangover. I just took a fabulous walk through the park. I love to watch toddlers racing around barefoot, climbing over each other like a litter of puppies and having the most fun. Kids are fantastic." She paused for a moment. "So were you last night, Ben."

"I loved being with you," the words slipped out of his

mouth. "I . . . I hope I helped in some way. What I mean is, seeing you in so much pain was awful!"

"That happens sometimes."

"I'm so sorry."

"Is that a turn-off for you?"

"Me? God, no!" Ben said. "MaryAnne, I'd love to see you, talk to you, watch you eat creepy-crawlies my people have disdained for millennia, get thrown out of restaurants, anything so long as you'll let me be with you."

She exploded with laughter. "Oysters are creepy-crawlies? You're hilarious!"

"Will that make up for my inability to come up with an inspirational message?"

There was another pause. "I assume you're up in Acadia?"

"Yes."

"How soon can you get here?"

WHEN BEN KNOCKED on her door exactly one hour and thirteen minutes later, a record for the fifty-mile drive, MaryAnne opened the door looking even lovelier than he remembered. She wore a brown sweater, beige pants and a chocolate newsboy cap, cocked over her left eye.

"You're a rhapsody in brown," was the best Ben could come up with.

"Are you looking for apartment 4202?" she played it so seriously he didn't know what she was talking about—at first. Then it dawned on him. "Peter told you about that disastrous blind date?"

"He did. How big a louse were you?"

"Pretty sizable, I guess. I should have handled it better. Do you hate me for that?"

"No. I'm actually glad you can be a swine sometimes. It makes you more accessible." Ben handed her the book he brought.

"The *Kabbalah*—in English!" She was like a little girl, excitedly flipping through the pages. "What a great gift! Thank you, thank you, thank you," She threw her arms around Ben's neck and kissed his face. She felt so good, he would have been happy to stand with her in the doorway all day.

Now that's a great gift!" Ben said and followed her into her apartment. "What else did Peter say about me?"

"You know he adores you. He thought the way you got out of that embarrassing situation was not only clever, but kind."

"When did he call you?"

"He didn't. I called him. I wanted to thank him for sending you to me."

Ben wanted to kiss her and he almost did when suddenly he noticed suitcases on the floor of the living room and his heart dropped. "Are you going somewhere?"

"Those are my roommate's. She just flew in from Vegas a couple of hours ago."

"How many roommates do you have?" Ben asked when a door opened and someone who looked like Sugar Ray Leonard came out with a towel around his waist.

"Hi," he smiled. "Where's the bathroom?"

"You're . . . ?" This man was obviously not her roommate.

"I'm LeMonde, Rita's friend. I really need to get to the bathroom."

"Second door past the kitchen."

MaryAnne watched him go into the bathroom. "She chose a cute one this time."

———

INSIDE HER BEDROOM, with books and notes strewn around her bed, MaryAnne explained that she had one roommate, Rita, a showgirl who worked in Las Vegas. She came to town every few weeks and it wasn't unusual to find strangers wandering in and out of her room at all hours.

"She never uses the kitchen, pays the rent in advance and is a kind person. I could do worse." MaryAnne plopped down on the bed in the middle of the books and papers, picked up her yellow pad and looked at the scribbling on it.

"A river runs through the Garden . . . ? What were we talking about last night?"

"Life, death, good, evil, friendship, loyalty, why we're on this planet, stuff like that."

"You make it sound like shop talk. Is that what it is for you?"

"Pretty much. What is it for you?"

"Foreplay."

BLISS WAS THE WORD that flowed out of Ben's deepest dream into his first waking moments. The sun was bursting through the gossamer curtain and the first thing that welcomed him was the sweet scent of her body. MaryAnne was up reading the *Kabbalah*. He wondered if she had slept at all. After their exhilarating love making, Ben passed out.

"*Le petit mort,*" she called it laughing, Ben watched as MaryAnne devoured the esoteric wisdom of the *Kabbalah* and in that moment, he allowed himself—no, he made himself—believe that she was going to be all right. Then he saw the array of pill bottles on her night table and gloom singed his brain once again. MaryAnne looked at Ben and smiled.

"Hi," he said. That was his way of saying I love you without the complications that accompany that phrase.

"Me, too," she smiled and kissed him and then read aloud from the book. ". . . preordained lovers are a single soul divided at birth. Their mission is to find their other half and when they do, they are rejoined and become one for all eternity. Therein lies their salvation."

She put down the book and rested on her elbow, her face practically touching Ben's. "So, when the heroes of *The Last of the Just* made love in the face of certain death, that was their salvation?"

"The mystics believe love is the gravitational force that keeps all elements of the cosmos in balance."

"What happens to that balance when one dies and the other doesn't?" MaryAnne was impatient to understand in an instant what others spend a lifetime studying, but the truth is that she comprehended the esoteric more thoroughly and more rapidly than anyone Ben had ever met.

"The *Kabbalah* describes in detail the complete change in Adam when he was suddenly granted God's greatest gift, his preordained soul mate. Through her, he understood the glories of love. He was alive and joyful in their magical garden. Fulfilling his mission to nourish the garden and procreate together with his *basherte* was his greatest delight."

Ben stretched his arms then continued. "That ended when tragedy struck. Eve died and Adam was so bereft, he lost all desire to continue to labor in the garden. The Heavenly Hosts feared that the newly created world, built to support a species created in the image of God, would collapse. They had good reason to be frightened. As it turned out, even God could not console Adam when he lost his soul mate. It wasn't only his rib that had been severed; it was his very soul that was withering inside him. Where was his other half? The part he could talk to without having to speak? Who would caress him and ease his burdens? God saw that life without one's true love was a curse every husband and wife after Adam and Eve would have to endure. The *Kabbalah* describes God's anguish in vivid detail as he watched Adam, who was '*inconsolable, with a heart that was ashen and eyes that took no pleasure in sight.*' God was so overwhelmed by Adam's grief that He created the river that flowed through the heart of Eden."

"That's the river you told me about last night!" The pieces were coming together for MaryAnne.

"The rabbis tell us that a mystical river flows directly from Eden into the hearts of all lovers everywhere, binding them for all eternity. The anguished, bereaved and spiritually wounded would bathe in those sparkling waters and literally pierce the veil to connect with their *bashert* on the other side. That is the balm that heals and enables them to go on."

"Where is that river, Ben? I have to know."

"It *will* be revealed, but only after one's mate passes through the river alone."

"What happens then?"

"The bereaved lover is magically transported to the holy river where their souls are reunited. There, as one, they regain the bliss and rapture they knew when they were alive, together and whole."

Her eyes were moist. "Do you believe that?"

"I want to," Ben held back his tears.

THE DAYS BLENDED INTO WEEKS, then into months. In the face of ever-increasing demands from Ben's congregation, his greatest challenge was figuring out what tasks and obligations he could avoid or postpone so that he could spend more time with MaryAnne. At the end of every workday, Ben raced into

Manhattan to be with his beloved and every morning he made the long trek back to Acadia. He was never so energized, so full of enthusiasm and optimism and, yes, so happy. MaryAnne was the single focus of his life. Ben must have given off some kind of vibration that made him appear impervious to petty stuff. The women in his book review program stopped trying to find him dates. Even Hank Sperling avoided pissing him off.

Ben and MaryAnne were enveloped in a magical universe. During those ecstatic days their love for one another gave them both wings. Sometimes there was a cough or stomach spasm that frightened him, but MaryAnne found ways to alleviate his fears.

Well into MaryAnne and Ben's fourth month together, Peter and Ben were having their weekly lunch at the club when Peter threw him a curve. "I understand MaryAnne is thinking about converting to Judaism," he said.

Ben was surprised. He and MaryAnne had been in each other's hearts and minds for exactly one hundred and eighteen days and Ben assumed he could read her every thought. He knew she was receptive to many of the ideas that derived from the *Kabbalah*. They discussed those often, but Ben had no inkling that she intended to convert and he wasn't sure how he felt about that. Why didn't she discuss it with him? Ben became uncharacteristically silent. Peter didn't know how to continue the discussion, so he remained silent. Finally, without looking at him, Ben asked, "When did you speak to her?"

"I didn't. I talked to her father briefly after the Sunday morning service and he told me he had been in touch with MaryAnne."

"He called her?"

"No. She called him."

"Why did she do that?"

"I couldn't say. She knew that her father was an outspoken anti-Semite and maybe she felt she owed it to him to be honest about her plan to convert to Judaism."

"Did she tell him anything else?"

"She said she was seeing a really nice guy," Peter said, faux conspiratorially. "Her father assumed it was a 'Hebrew,' so he didn't want to hear about it and she didn't volunteer any names, if that's what you're asking."

"Did she tell him anything about herself?"

Peter took another long sip of his martini. "She told him she had left the show and mentioned that she was taking a battery of tests at Mount Sinai Hospital."

"Did the anti-Semitic bastard at least ask what kind of tests?"

"I'm sure he sensed something wasn't kosher, pun intended. I don't know if it scared him or if he just doesn't like to hear bad news. In any event, he didn't ask for specifics and she didn't offer any. He told her to steer clear of hospitals because they're full of sick people and that he didn't trust doctors. His advice was to eat right and get plenty of exercise."

"Didn't he at least ask what was going on with his daughter? Did he want to know how she was feeling, if he could help—all the things any normal father would want to know?"

Peter shook his head.

"What a *putz!*"

"Yeah, you can say that again."

That night, when Ben arrived at her door, MaryAnne knew something was up. "You look unusually glum, Ben. What's going on?" Ben hadn't mentioned Peter or that he knew about the conversation with her father. He didn't have to. MaryAnne could take one look at Ben and know everything he was thinking.

"It's not like I would have to undergo circumcision," MaryAnne said trying to lighten the mood.

"But it is a major step," Ben said.

"Everything is at this point," MaryAnne replied softly. They generally avoided that conversation, but when it emerged, those words sent waves of anxiety shooting through Ben's body. She held his hand, kissed it and stared into his eyes. "Ben, this is not a desperate last-minute attempt to get in good with the God of your patriarchs. I've been thinking about it for quite a while. I'm still thinking about it and when I make a decision, if I do, you'll be the first to know. The one thing I want you to understand is that it's all about living, not dying, okay?"

"Okay," Ben said and realized that every moment he had with MaryAnne, *was* okay.

After months of daily commutes. Ben became an ace pathfinder. He figured out the best routes and the best hours to avoid the heavy traffic. Ben liked to share those minor triumphs with MaryAnne between lovemaking, studying, walking, talking and dancing. He didn't mention that particular conversation again. Nor did she.

Ben finally met MaryAnne's roommate, Rita. One day when he arrived early, MaryAnne was out shopping for groceries and a willowy woman nearly six feet tall with a cascade of scarlet hair came out of the second bedroom. She explained that she was a dancer at The Riviera in Las Vegas and her job was essentially to walk up and down stairs onstage clad in an enormous headpiece, sparkling jewels and not much else. She felt she was more suited to acting than dancing, but ". . . it's so hard to get a tit in the door." She laughed at the joke she had obviously told many times before.

When she returned, Ben was never happier to see MaryAnne. "I don't know how to talk to Rita," he groused.

"I don't imagine she'd be any more interested in your synagogue business than you are in her career, but as I told you before, she's a good soul and the perfect roommate. She's not here much so that's good, but when she is here she's considerate and she genuinely loves people."

"I know. I counted three of them using the bathroom last night."

He promised MaryAnne he'd try to be less judgmental, but Rita was the first Vegas showgirl he had ever met and he found her ways—challenging. When he did try to engage Rita in conversation, no matter what topic they started on, he always wound up feeling like the straight man for a burlesque joke. Worse were the times that Rita confided in him about intimate problems of being a showgirl—or regaled him with stories about men with odd Italian nicknames who liked to take people for drives in the desert. The fact that someone as sophisticated and erudite as MaryAnne was able to connect with Rita demonstrated once again that she had evolved way beyond Ben's narrow mindset.

"I bet you can communicate with anyone, even animals," he joked.

"Doesn't everyone?" she asked innocently.

BY THE END of their eighth month, it became more and more difficult to ignore what was going on. MaryAnne felt tired much of the time and she had little energy. The slightest exertion exhausted her. Ben went with her to visit her oncologist, a compassionate man who was from his parents' generation. The doctor spoke in gentle and encouraging terms but made no attempt to hide the facts. He said that some people with MaryAnne's condition do exceed expectations, but the odds were not in her favor and they should be prepared for all contingencies. Neither Ben nor MaryAnne were willing to hear that. They were determined to beat this thing.

The following week MaryAnne took a turn for the worse. Ben got a call in his study from Mount Sinai Hospital telling him that MaryAnne had fallen in the bathtub and was now in the intensive care unit. Rita had found her and called an ambulance. At the hospital, she had given them his number. Ben dropped everything and raced down the Cross Bronx Expressway. When he walked into her room he nearly fell on the floor when he saw her hooked up to machines monitoring her vital signs with tubes plugged in everywhere.

Forcing himself upright, he walked to MaryAnne's side. Her eyes were closed. He stood beside her bed and prayed like he'd never prayed before. He felt the air whooshing out of his body and became light headed. An alert orderly saw him swaying and he quickly pulled Ben out of the ICU and into the hallway where he put him in a hard wooden chair and made him sit with his head between his knees until the fog cleared.

The next three days were the most miserable and desolate of Ben's life. The radiology reports revealed that the cancer had invaded her colon and both ovaries and was spreading to her kidneys and liver. When she regained consciousness, she held onto Ben's hand as tightly as she could.

"Ben . . ." she had difficulty speaking. "You have to something for me."

"What is it?"

"I've been searching all my life and I finally discovered who I am. I am not a yogi. I'm not a New Age flower child. I am Tevya's daughter, the Jewish girl you fell in love with."

"I fell in love with *you*. It doesn't matter to me if . . ."

She held up her hand. "Please, Ben. I've made the most important decision of my life and you have to help me."

"Anything," Ben said.

"I've decided—I want to become a Jew. Will you do that for me?"

"I'll do anything you ask, but you have to do something for me."

"If I can."

"Marry me."

"I can do that," she said and they both wept.

Peter was the only one Ben thought of calling. Later that evening, he arrived with a pleasant looking, middle-aged woman he introduced as Margaret Stanton, a member of his parish who was a District Court judge. Judge Stanton had brought a marriage license to be filled out. All MaryAnne and Ben had to do was sign and she would take care of the rest. After Ben and MaryAnne did that, the judge said she would be honored to remain for the ceremony and act as a witness. Ben embraced her.

Peter wrapped a *tallit* around Ben's shoulders and handed him the *Rabbi's Manual*. Ben opened it and read, "'. . . and Ruth said: Entreat me not to leave you and to return from following after you; for wherever you go, I will go; and where you lie down, there will I lie. Your people will be my people and your God, my God.' Welcome dear MaryAnne, to the faith of Moses and Israel. May you grow in strength and stature alongside Sarah, Rebecca, Rachel, and Leah and all the other great daughters of Zion."

"Amen," Peter said. Ben turned several pages of the manual and handed it to Peter.

"*B'ruchim Ha-baim,*" Peter began in Hebrew, and then switched to English. "Blessed be you, MaryAnne and Ben, who come together this day to be joined in holy matrimony. May your souls be bound together in the bonds of eternal love and devotion to one another."

Looking at Ben, he said, "You may place the ring on the hand of your betrothed."

Ben placed the ring on MaryAnne's finger. "With this ring, I thee wed. Be thou consecrated unto me as my wife for all eternity." He kissed his bride.

"*Mazal tov!*" Peter proclaimed. "According to the laws of Moses and Israel and the State of New York, I pronounce you man and wife, co-travelers through life and beyond. May your love be an inspiration and a blessing."

A month after they were married, Ben stood at her gravesite. The plot was on a high hill with a perfect view of the Hudson River. He remained there until the sun set. During that entire afternoon Ben felt himself awash in the river that ran through their souls and remembered the question she had asked on their first meeting. "Where exactly was Eden?" Ben didn't know the answer then, but he did now. Wherever MaryAnne was, there was Eden.

for the love of bertha

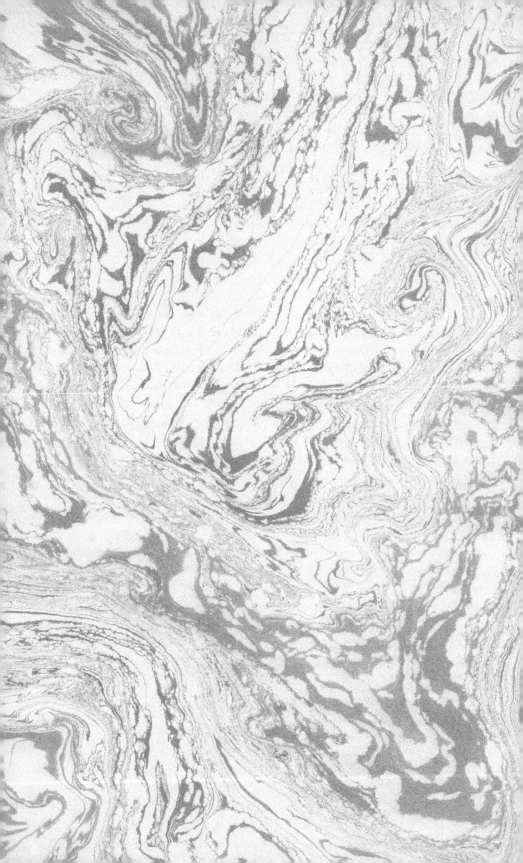

1989.

BERTHA WAS EXCITED. "The Kosher Luncheon Club is offering a free trip to Sidneyland—I mean Disneyland! We leave by
bus at eight in the morning. They provide a light breakfast with
coffee and donuts. Who needs their donuts? I'll bring my own
bagels. We can go on all the rides free, even the roller-toaster,
then lunch. It will be dairy, but that's all right . . ."

Seeing his mother so energized and involved in a variety
of activities that took her mind off her very real aches and
pains validated all the trouble Ben had gone through to convince her to move to California. Ben's father died more than
twenty years ago and his mother's life in Youngstown had been
steadily shrinking. For a while, Bertha had a part time job at

May's department store as a saleslady in coats. She made a few friends and enjoyed talking to browsing shoppers three afternoons a week. She received minimum wage, but her needs were minimal and together with her social security checks she was able to maintain the lifestyle she preferred, which meant depriving herself of even minor luxuries so that she could send generous gifts to her children and grandchildren on their birthdays and holidays.

Bertha's manageable lifestyle ended abruptly three months ago when May's decided to go out of business. The prospect of Bertha sitting home alone every day, with nothing to do but stare at the walls in her dark living room, was depressing beyond words.

Ben had recently been installed as rabbi of Temple Har Zion, a prestigious synagogue in Los Angeles, and he decided that this would be an opportune time for his mother to move to California. With most of her friends and relatives either dead or dying, he couldn't let her sit home alone becoming more despondent every day, so he flew to Youngstown to convince her to make the move.

Bertha was so glum when Ben arrived that she barely said a word, which for her was a serious symptom. He assumed she would greet his offer with enthusiasm, but Bertha had reservations.

"Benny I would love nothing more than to live with you in your new Temple," she explained, "but let's face facts. I'm not prepared to be 'the rabbi's mother.' Your members will ask me to advise about the holidays, the Bible, all kinds things. What do I know? Nothing."

"Mom, do you expect your doctor's mother to know how to read an X-ray, or your accountant's mother to file tax returns?"

"Uncle Jake does my taxes," Bertha said. She wasn't evading

the issue. For Ben's mother, the issue was whatever popped into her head. "Bennele, listen to me. The people in your temple are educated. All I ever had was a couple years of night school when I came to America. The worst part is I never even became a naturalized citizen. People will think the rabbi's mother is a stupid."

"People will not think that, Mom, and if they do, they can kiss my *touchus*."

"I never liked that expression, but somehow when you say it, it doesn't sound so bad." Bertha couldn't look at Ben without *kvelling*. "Such a beautiful boy," she pinched his cheek.

"Move to California and you can pinch to your heart's content."

"Benny, darling, there's another thing. Daddy is buried twenty minutes by bus. I visit him whenever I want to talk out the heart. What will I do when I'm so far away?"

"You can talk to Daddy wherever you are. You know that, mom, don't you?"

"I know, I know. Still, it's hard. Daddy was so smart. He always knew what was the right thing to do."

"Mom ... did you ever ask Daddy about the possibility of moving in a totally new direction?" Ben had heard that romance often blossoms among senior citizens and quite a few of them end up remarrying. He thought that would be a great idea for Bertha. She was gregarious, craved company and was attractive enough to snag a friendly widower.

"I don't understand."

"Maybe Dad would want you to travel, meet new people. Who knows, maybe even meet a nice man?"

Her mouth dropped open. "I should cheat on your father? From the day I met Daddy, I never looked at another man. Please God, strike me dead first."

"Okay, Mom. Sorry I brought it up." He should have realized that was a difficult concept to consider in the abstract.

Bertha continued to steam. "What am I, *meshugah* altogether? I should bring a strange man I don't even know into my house? They'll want to boss me around and control my TV remote. I won't even be able to watch my programs!"

"As far as the TV goes, people make compromises."

"I should compromise with some slob who dirties up my house and leaves laundry on the floor and snores so loud he wakes up the whole neighborhood?"

"Who does that?"

"My neighbor's new husband, Nick the bum. You remember I told you about the nice Italian lady who moved in next door? Such an angel! She's living through hell, excuse me. She says her children told her they got a message from their dead father, you know, from the other side, that he wanted she should remarry. They found an old friend of the husband who was a widower, looking for a wife. He told her he got the same message so they figured it was meant to be. Everybody said this Nick was a nice guy and she didn't mind him hanging around, but after they got married, no more Mr. Nice Guy. This bum turned into the biggest *stronzo*."

"Do you know what that word means in Italian?"

"Not exactly, but I figure it's plenty bad."

"I guess somebody got the wrong signals from the other side," Ben said.

"So how do you know which message is real and which one is baloney?"

"You feel it in your stomach, Mom."

Bertha became uncharacteristically silent. Tears filled the corners of her eyes.

"What's wrong, Mom?"

"I got suddenly a *knitch* in my stomach," Bertha said. "It happens sometimes when I know what a person is telling me is right but I'm afraid to hear it. Bennele, you think I don't know what a fool I am for not taking you up on your nice offer to bring me to California? You want to know the truth? I would love to live near you. What I'm afraid of is that with your mother there to do your cooking and cleaning you'll never get married again. Your MaryAnne told you she didn't want you to be alone and if I was the reason you didn't find a nice girl it would break my heart for sure."

"Listen to your stomach," Ben said. "It's madness for you to sit here alone all day and stare at the walls. You will have your own apartment. We can talk on the phone every day, but I'll have my privacy and if I want to go out on dates, nothing's holding me back."

AFTER THE FIRST FEW WEEKS of doubt and misgivings, Bertha began to find her way around Los Angeles. Her apartment was bigger than her entire house in Youngstown and sunnier, with a huge bay window.

"I look out and wave to the neighborhood kids when they walk by and you know what? They wave back!" Bertha couldn't contain her excitement. "Green grass grows everywhere and my street is lined with tall palm trees on both sides."

When Sam the kosher butcher brought her a free chicken to celebrate her first Shabbat in Los Angeles, she was happier than she had been in years. "Everybody in California is so friendly!"

She couldn't remember the nice things she experienced all at once, so she called Ben three, four times a day to tell him what good times she was having. "I got a free senior citizens bus pass! My new next-door neighbor, Harriet—that's a woman's name? Anyhow, Harry took me to the YWCA and enrolled me in the free senior swimming classes . . ."

Bertha was more enthusiastic than she had been in years. She had people to talk to. She was somebody. The first Friday evening when she came to the synagogue, the president of the temple, Sidney Edelman, made a point of welcoming her from the pulpit as an honorary member and everyone applauded. Bertha absolutely glowed.

The *piece de résistance* was an invitation to join the Ladies' Auxiliary of Temple Har Zion as an honorary member. "So many friendly women and they all said they wanted to get to know me and how much they loved my son, the handsome, young rabbi." Bertha had no idea why the women were so solicitous, but Ben did—and he didn't think it was something he should discuss with her just yet.

In Los Angeles, as in previous pulpits, there were women who saw a widowed rabbi as a perfect match for one of the divorced, widowed or otherwise available women in the community. When Ben's mother arrived, they thought they had found the perfect ally to encourage him to choose one of their daughters to remarry. What they didn't manage to convey was that she should support their recommendations and not go out fishing on her own, but Bertha was friendly to everyone. If she met a girl in the supermarket who was attractive and had a nice smile, she would flash a picture of her son, the single rabbi. Soon, she was getting calls from dozens of available women all over West Los Angeles, Beverly Hills and Santa Monica.

At their weekly Sunday morning brunch, Bertha would read off the latest list of possible dates. Ben's reaction didn't please her. "It's not normal, Benny. A single man, especially one that's brilliant and gorgeous like you, can't make time to go out with a pretty young girl every so often? I'm not saying you have to get married right away or even go steady, but if that should happen, what would be so terrible?"

"It's complicated," Ben explained. "Everybody who sees me with a girl will want to know what's going on, why *her* and not *my* daughter, why *her* and not *me*? Is she Jewish? What kind of family does she come from? Am I serious? Is she divorced, a widow, a virgin or what?"

"So you'll never have a date?" Bertha couldn't hide her disapproval "You'll sit home alone and lock yourself in the bathroom and make noises like a twelve year old?"

"Lock myself in the bathroom? What are you saying?"

"Me? Nothing," Bertha looked away and sipped her tea. "My friend Ida from Akron says all young boys lock themselves in the bathroom and do things before they're old enough to go out on dates."

"What kind of things?"

"How would I know? So tell me, Benny, what did you eat for lunch today?"

LOS ANGELES PROVIDES a variety of social, cultural and educational opportunities for seniors and Bertha joined more clubs in her first month in L.A. than she had all the years she lived in Youngstown. She went to the Westwood Seniors coffee klatch every Tuesday, the kosher luncheon at the Federation on Wednesday, water aerobics on Thursday and a host of other activities that were available twenty-four, seven.

"The Sunshine Club is offering a bus trip to Las Vegas with a free stay in a fancy hotel. What do you think, Benny, should I go?"

"Why not? It will be a totally new experience for you, mom, that I promise, but it's a pretty long drive."

"That's okay, I like long bus rides. The old men in the group say Las Vegas is where all the hot young girls are. Is that true?"

"I'm sure there are hot young girls everywhere," Ben said with one eye on the football game on TV. "Is that what you're looking for?"

"Me? No. But if you wanted to come along, maybe you could meet a nice young woman and have yourself a date, for a change."

"Sorry, I can't get away but I see no reason why you shouldn't go. I'm sure you'll have a good time."

When Bertha returned from Las Vegas, she couldn't contain her enthusiasm. "Such a city, bright lights on every street, big fountains and flowers everywhere you look, and the hotel! Don't ask. They were such sports. As soon as the bus pulled up, the hotel manager gave each of us a twenty-dollar chip so we could gamble. Isn't that something? And the girls! So pretty and friendly. I met one by the elevator, such a pleasant girl. She would go right up to a man and ask him if he wanted a date. Girls would never be so forward in my day. You should go there. I'm telling you, in Las Vegas you'll have all the dates you want and you don't have to be afraid somebody will see you having a good time. Oh! I didn't tell you. I also made money."

"You gambled?"

"Of course not. What am I, *meshugah*? Everybody who gambled lost money."

"So what did you do, find a date at the elevator and get a tip from some high roller?"

"Don't talk foolish."

Ben wondered if his mother knew what those women meant when they asked men at the elevators if they wanted a "date." He hoped she didn't and he was glad his mother didn't ask, but he *was* curious about how she came away making money.

"I watched some of the high risers in the group play slot machines, but I didn't see the sense in that. Why leave the lounge where everybody was so sociable, to go sit alone with a machine that swallows up your money? The pretty cocktail waitresses with the nice long legs brought me plenty of free cokes and seltzer and all kinds snacks and when it was time to come home, since I didn't gamble, I cashed in the twenty dollar chip."

"Amazing, Mom, You beat the system."

"And I had such a good time! Everybody was so nice. Wherever you go in Las Vegas there are people to talk to. You know, Benny, it's important to have somebody to talk out the heart."

"Yes, Mom, I talk to people all day."

"But I'm not talking about work. Some of these girls are saints. If you heard what they've been through, it would break your heart. One had a husband who ran away with her sister and then came back. Now all three of them live together in her trailer and she supports everybody including some kids from another marriage. They asked me for advice. What could I tell them? I said respect yourself and be honest with everybody, even people you don't like."

"Sounds like good advice, Mom"

"That's what one of the pretty young girls with a nice figure told me. They all said how much they enjoyed talking to me. Isn't that something? Anyway, I brought you these."

Bertha whipped out a stack of snap shots. "The hotel gave us disposable cameras so I took some pictures." She handed Ben a packet filled with promotional material and advertisements for

"Hotel Extravaganza Night" *and* eighteen four-by-five photographs of Bertha's idea of nice, friendly girls.

"The hotel developed the pictures for us while they served a huge luncheon. So much food! Who can eat all that? Most of it was un-kosher stuff, but they also had fruit and cottage cheese and . . ." Bertha recited the entire menu, from salads and appetizers to desserts and soft drinks in exhaustive detail as Ben perused the snap shots. On the back of each photo was a name, a phone number and a few personal words addressed to Bertha. There were showgirls, cocktail waitresses and aspiring actresses. Some of them wrote that in the event Bertha knew any agents, they were available for all roles, large and small *and* would consider *some* frontal nudity. Ben was grateful that there weren't any female impersonators. At least, he didn't think there were and he didn't want to get into that discussion with his mother.

"Nice, huh?" Bertha said, hopefully

"Yeah, Mom. I'm glad you made so many new friends."

She was obviously disappointed that Ben wasn't more enthusiastic. "Benny, you're still young and you're plenty busy right now, but the years go by so fast you don't even notice. Before you realize it you'll be old and that's when you'll understand how lonely life can be. Bennele, Bennele, you've had enough grief in your young life. Don't you think MaryAnne would want you to be happy? It's time you had some *fargeneigen*. Look through the pictures again, darling. What can it hurt? You might decide you want to call up one of the pretty girls."

At their next Sunday brunch, Bertha mentioned that she had been in contact with some of her new "Vegas friends" and one in particular was planning to visit Los Angeles in a couple of weeks.

"That's great, Mom," Ben really liked that idea. Visitors for her meant he could watch football on TV while his mother entertained her guest.

Bertha didn't mention it again for several days, but the following Sunday she brought it up again. "You remember I told you about my friend, Sonia, from Las Vegas? She'll be in town next weekend. Would it be all right to invite her to join us for brunch?"

"Of course." Ben was genuinely happy to have someone else around with whom she could "talk out the heart." Bertha needed to talk far more than Ben wished to listen, so he was delighted to share her with as many friends as she could find.

"There's a playoff game on TV I'd like to see," Ben said. "Do you think your guest would mind if I watched it?"

"Why should she mind? Of course it would be nice if you would say a few words and don't sit there like a couch tomato."

"Potato, Mom. Couch *potato*, and yes, I will be civil," Ben promised. "I'll even try to be charming."

She grabbed Ben's cheek and squeezed. "Such a *punim*! Are you kidding me? My Bennele is the most charming man in America."

America, for Bertha, took precedence over the planet or the universe. She had her own set of prayers, which usually began with thanking God for America, the home of the brave and the free, and ended with a special plea to God. "Please find a nice girl for my Bennele—he should live and be well for many years—and they should get married and raise a beautiful, healthy family, *o-meyn*."

The following Sunday morning when Ben knocked on Bertha's door an extremely attractive young woman greeted him. She was slender with long espresso-brown hair, an aristocratic nose and a smile that took his breath away.

"You must be Ben," she said in a mellifluous voice that matched her dazzling looks.

This gorgeous girl couldn't be . . . Ben was flummoxed. "Are you Mom's friend from Las Vegas?" he asked when he was finally able to put words together.

She looked him over. "I don't know why, but I imagined you would be taller."

"You're not what I expected, either," Ben said.

"What *were* you expecting?" She said with a glint in her eye.

"Someone thirty or forty years older, for one thing." Wow, this girl is some beauty, Ben thought. With looks like that, she must make a killing in Vegas. Was she a lap-dancer, hooker or showgirl?

Bertha came out of the kitchen and gave Ben her usual warm embrace and cheerful smile. "Did I lie to you, Sonia? Is my Bennele gorgeous or what?"

"Gorgeous isn't the word I'd choose, Bertha," she said looking him over. "He's more—intellectual-looking, respectable. The word I'd choose would be—dignified."

"I know," Bertha beamed. "He was always a smart one but who knew he'd grow up to be so dignified?"

Ben felt his nose drift a little off kilter. Intellectual looking, respectable and dignified were simply not the same as gorgeous. He followed his mother and her guest into the dining area where Ben usually set the table. He was surprised to find that it was already set. Bertha proudly announced that her new friend had done all the work. "Isn't Sonia the sweetest thing? She won't let me lift a finger. She wants me to sit down and relax while she makes brunch. And so pretty! I could look at her all day."

Mom was right, Ben had to admit. Sonia was stunning, but he couldn't figure her out. She pretended not to have any interest in him, but why would she come all the way from Las Vegas to visit his mother if not to stake a claim on the available rabbi? Ben turned on the TV. The Forty-Niners had just kicked off but he couldn't get into the game. He kept thinking about Sonia. She looked so familiar. He had seen here before. But where?

Ben walked to the kitchen and looked in. Bertha and her guest seemed to be sharing a moment as they laughed and talked in hushed tones. "Excuse me for interrupting," Ben said, "but you look very familiar, Sonia. Do I know you?"

"My name isn't Sonia, it's Soji," she said. "I didn't correct your mother because it sounds so cute the way she says it."

Soji . . . Soji . . . "Are you Soji Mack?" Ben asked. How could he not recognize Soji Mack, the Scream Queen? A devoted fan of gothic horror flicks, Ben must have seen every one of her films.

"In the flesh."

Her reference to "flesh" evoked the many times Ben had watched her lithe body being menaced by everything from psychopaths to aliens. "I've seen your movies," Ben said. "They're classics. I especially loved *Beyond Evil.*"

Soji couldn't have been less interested.

Bertha was curious. "What's Behind Evil?"

Soji laughed out loud. "Behind Evil! That would have been a much better title. It's equally inane, but it has a comic twist to it. If only my producers had your sense of humor, Bertha," she said and hugged her.

"So, Behind Evil is a movie?" Bertha wasn't sure she got it right.

"It's a movie Soji starred in that was a huge hit," Ben explained.

Bertha smiled at Soji. Her belief in her new friend was now completely validated. "Sonia, are you a famous actress? Why didn't somebody tell me? Better yet, why didn't I guess a young girl as beautiful and nice as you, why shouldn't you be a movie star? Isn't that exciting, Benny? I didn't even know my nice friend was a celebrity. How can a person be so beautiful and so modest? Have you ever met anyone like her? The truth, Benny. Have you ever?"

Ben didn't answer but he knew his mother well enough that it didn't matter what anybody else thought. When she liked someone, they were her friend for life.

"Are you still making movies?" Ben asked.

"No, I gave that up two years ago."

"And moved to Vegas to . . . ?"

"It's a long story."

"Is there a short version?"

"I'm a financial advisor. I deal mainly in off-shore investments."

"Sounds exciting."

"That's not the word I'd choose," she said.

"How about intellectual, respectable or dignified?"

"You're funnier than I thought you would be," she said.

"But still not gorgeous," Ben parried.

"No, but funny is good."

Ben was more interested than he thought he would be. "Speaking of funny, is Soji your real name, or is that something a press agent dreamed up?"

"I was named after Sojourner Truth," she said, "an early feminist and abolitionist. My parents were devout members of Arbiter Ring, Jewish Trotskyites."

"How do they feel about you laboring in the vineyards of the capitalists?"

"They're both dead, so I don't think they feel too much of anything, or am I wrong about that, Rabbi?"

"Sonia, how many eggs, darling?" Bertha stood over the stove.

"Six, Bertha," Soji blushed and said quietly "I don't remember my own mother ever calling me darling."

Ben was puzzled as he walked back to the Barcalounger. What is this girl's agenda? He tried to focus on the game but heard them laughing in the kitchen. Soji was apparently showing Bertha how to make a special kind of omelet stuffed with fruit.

"Ben loves new dishes, don't you Bennele?" Bertha yelled out. "Remember when I made you the tuna bake? They say it looked like those fish cakes some people make from crabs that crawl around like bugs, but mine were kosher and delicious. You loved it, Remember?"

Ben was used to not responding to Bertha's ongoing monologues, so he said nothing.

A moment later, Soji came into the living room holding a spatula. "Your mother asked you if you remember her tuna bake."

"I heard her."

"You didn't say anything, so I thought you didn't."

"Soji, I don't know how well you know my mother. She's a lovely person but she never stops talking. I care deeply about her, but if I have to listen to her endless prattle I will go nuts. I want to continue to spend as much time with her as I can, but in order for me to do that we had to establish certain ground rules."

"Rules? Defining what your mother can talk about and when?"

"It's not as draconian as all that. Anytime she's troubled or has something important she wants to discuss, I'm always there for her. It's just the continuous prattle that I can't deal with."

"I see," Soji said with an edge of sarcasm. "The fact that

your mother tries to engage you in a discussion about dishes she hopes will please you is not important enough to distract you from your football game. Gotcha."

Soji went back into the kitchen without another word. Ben thought of following her to elaborate on what he meant. Instead, he decided that the best way for her to understand his predicament was to wait until she'd had an earful of Bertha's nonstop chatter. *We'll see how much she can handle before she plugs her ears.* He continued to watch the game but kept the volume low so that he could hear them in the kitchen. He was surprised that so little was said about him. Bertha explained why she didn't recognize Soji's name because, first of all, she doesn't go to movies much since her husband died and that was over twenty years ago and they don't make movies the way they used to anyway. Then, without stopping to make a connection she continued. "My best friend who was maid of honor at my wedding, we got married in Akron, her name was Sonia, too!"

Ben expected Soji to run for the door after that characteristic dose of Bertha's free association, but she didn't. She laughed and said "Bertha, you're priceless!"

AT THE TABLE, BERTHA DISCOVERED how much Soji paid for a hotel the previous night and she was outraged. "It's a crime to throw away money on a hotel when you can sleep here. After brunch, let's go get your things and you can move in with me. Please Sonia, that would make me so happy."

Ben nearly choked on his omelet. *A former B-movie queen from Vegas staying with the rabbi's mother?* The Temple Sisterhood would burn her house down.

"That's so sweet, Bertha, but I have to fly back to Vegas

tonight. I've got tons of work to do. I came in to see you and to attend a party in honor of a good friend and client."

"A party?" Bertha brightened up. "Benny, how long has it been since you went to a party?"

Soji smiled at Ben. "Would you like to come?"

"Sorry, I've got a funeral in about two hours and a wedding this evening," Ben said. "What kind of party is it?"

"Ernie Fryberg's birthday. Do you know him?"

"Not personally," Ben said. *Ernie Fryberg?! The billionaire junk-bond king?* "I read somewhere that he was serving time in a European jail," Ben said, trying not to sound supercilious.

"Ernie was at a Swiss government restricted facility for ten months," Soji said, "but he's back now and his friends are throwing him a bash this afternoon at the Playboy Mansion. Sure you wouldn't like to come?" she asked with a wry smile.

Would I like to go to a party at the Playboy Mansion? A kaleidoscope of centerfolds spun in Ben's mind. He hadn't been with a woman since—MaryAnne. Ben found solace in working long hours, often seven days a week. However, he couldn't say he wasn't tempted. The thought of taking off an afternoon to be surrounded by the sexiest women on the planet was an image he couldn't allow himself to even fantasize about. "I really wish I could," was the best he could come up with, "but unfortunately . . ."

"What about you, Bertha?" Soji asked. "Would you like to come?"

"Me? I haven't been to a party in years. I wouldn't know what to wear," Bertha said as she twisted the napkin she was holding.

"It's very casual." Soji insisted. "Most of the action will be around the pool. What you're wearing is fine; just take off the apron. Or, leave it on. This is Hollywood, anything goes."

Soji shot a teasing smile in Ben's direction. "Sure you don't want to stop by for a quick dip, Ben?"

"You have no idea how much I would love that," he said. "Unfortunately I can't, but why don't you go, Mom?"

"You think I should?"

"Sure, you'll enjoy it."

"You know, Benny. Maybe you're right. So what should I wear to a Hollywood party?" Bertha headed into her bedroom, listing her clothing choices out loud.

"That was nice of you Ben," Soji said after they heard the door shut, "and don't worry. I promise to bring Mom home before ten. I won't let her drink or do drugs."

Ben couldn't help but smile. *This woman is bewitching me. Wait, what's she up to with this "Mom" business?* He decided to change the subject and see how she reacted.

"So, how well do you know Ernie Fryberg?" Ben finally asked. This time he didn't mind sounding supercilious.

"I handle some of his off-shore investments."

Ernie Fryberg keeps this Vegas beauty around to handle his investments? Ben had to control himself to keep from smirking. He had heard stories about how fat, bald Ernie traveled with at least a dozen gorgeous girls. He bought them thousands of dollars-worth of clothes and jewelry, but it gave him the right to enter their unlocked rooms at any hour of the day or night. He wondered if Ernie had the same arrangement with his "investment counselor."

Just then, Bertha came out of her bedroom dressed in a simple white jump suit with yellow embroidery. "You look lovely, Bertha," Soji said.

"I was just going to say that!" Ben groused. Soji trumped him again!

———————

BEN LEFT THE WEDDING immediately after the ceremony so that he could get home and call Bertha. He was eager to find out how her party at the Playboy Mansion turned out. Ben hoped his mother hadn't exposed herself—and him—to ridicule by going to a party where people allegedly swam nude and who knew what else?

No answer. It was ten o'clock! Where could she be? Bertha never stayed out late unless she was with him. Ben started to work on an article for the temple newsletter that was due the next day, but he couldn't concentrate. He called a few more times and finally, after eleven, she picked up.

Bertha was so excited. "What a lovely party!" and she launched into a detailed list of every dish that was served.

"Did you meet Ernie's Fryberg's mother?" Ben had heard that she went everywhere with him.

"I did," Bertha said. "What a nice little woman. Thelma's her name," and she proceeded to tell Ben everything they talked about. He didn't have to hear specifics. He had often seen the duet of two aging mothers bragging about the sons they adored, talking endlessly at one another without pause, neither listening to what the other one said. They would wait until one of them had to catch their breath, then jump in again. It wasn't really a competition; each had won in her own mind before they even began. If you were to ask either mother about the other's son, their answer would be: "He's nice, but where does he come to my son?"

"And that Sonia, what a doll," Bertha raved. "She took me all around the house. A regular mansion, I'm telling you. What a big place, so interesting with all the paintings and statues and tapestries, *Gottenyu!* Must be worth a fortune. Sonia didn't want to leave me alone for a minute, but I finally convinced her to go swimming with the young people. Boy oh boy, you should see what she looks like in a bathing suit. She is some beauty!"

He knew, and so did several million other people who had seen her movies. Soji Mack was one sexy girl.

"Anyway, it was a wonderful party. Did I tell you Sonia introduced me to everyone as her second mother? Isn't she something? I'm sorry she has to work in Las Vegas, otherwise I could see her every day. She called me her second mother, did I tell you that?"

"Yes you did, mom."

"I only wish she was my daughter."

Ben found himself feeling conflicted. Mom thinks of Soji as a daughter? He couldn't stop thinking of her in a bathing suit.

During the next week, Bertha raved about her new "daughter" who called her long distance every night.

"How much do you know about her?" Ben asked.

"I know she's had a hard life. Her own mother never showed any affection. Her parents were *farbrente* communists. They treated the poor child like a soldier and made her go on protest marches where people threw garbage at her. Her first husband was cruel and spiteful. She had to work night and day to get rid of the louse. She ended up paying him off plenty just to leave her alone. Did you ever hear such a thing? It's a crying shame. Such a sweet girl and she's had so much *tzuris* in her young life. Did you talk to her? She is such a good soul, she deserves better. Maybe, with God's help, she'll find a good man to take care of her."

"Mom?"

"Yes, darling?"

"This man you hope will look after Soji. You're not thinking of anyone in particular, are you?"

"Anyone in particular? You mean you? You think I'm trying to fix Sonia up with you?"

"The thought had occurred to me," Ben said.

"Please, Benny, don't make me out to be some kind of schemer. When I first came out to California, I tried to find you a date. I didn't want people should say your mother's in town so you'll have somebody to look after you, the sad widower who won't think any more about getting married.

"You said, no, so I stopped looking. I brought you pictures of some of the nice girls I met in Las Vegas, just for a date—not even anything serious. You said, no, again. I finally learned, no is no. You're a beautiful man, my Bennele, and any girl you end up with will be the luckiest person in America, but who am I to say who that person should be? Sonia is my friend. I love her and she loves me, but that has nothing to do with you, my handsome prince."

He was glad they cleared that up. That should have come as a relief. It didn't.

He waited for Bertha to continue talking. She didn't.

"Are you all right, mom?" Ben asked after a couple moments of rare silence.

"Yes dear," she said but she sounded distracted. "There was something I wanted to ask Sonia, but I forgot."

"Call her." Ben said.

"She said she'd be out late tonight. I'll call her tomorrow when she gets back to Las Vegas."

Out? Ben steamed silently. Who would she be out with so late? Didn't she have to take a plane back to Vegas tonight? Where could she be—and why did his mother have to tell him that?!

WHEN BEN ARRIVED FOR BRUNCH the next Sunday, there was a note attached to the screen door. It was signed by Soji and his heart started to beat faster.

"Ben, please enter quietly. I'm guiding Mom through a meditation."

Ben reread the note. *"Mom!"* That suggested joint possession as though they were part of a triangle. Were they? Ben wished she'd be a little more forthcoming, at least give him some clue as to whether she thinks about him at all. Bertha said Soji wasn't trying to nab him but what if she's wrong? He wouldn't put it past this girl to exploit his mother's naiveté to get to her son. If that were what she was thinking, it would be truly reprehensible. On the other hand . . . Soji was an unusually beautiful woman and, yes, he would probably like it if she showed even the slightest interest in him, but that was beside the point. Wait. What was the point?

Ben stood at the door staring at her note. "Guiding Mom through a meditation?" *Excuse me! There already is a spiritual guide in this family,* Ben bristled. Why didn't Soji lead *him* through a meditation? Better yet, why doesn't she ask him to lead *her* through one?

All this flashed through Ben's cluttered mind as he quietly entered the house. Bertha and Soji were sitting cross-legged opposite one another. His mother's eyes were closed. When Soji saw Ben, she raised her finger to her lips. Ben had to admit that his mother looked more relaxed than she had in years, but then, relaxation wasn't one of Bertha's defining traits. She always seemed to be in a state of heightened anxiety. Ben couldn't remember ever seeing her sit in one place very long. She was either popping up to bring another dish to the table or rummaging through letters to show Ben the latest pictures of his nieces and nephew, or shuffling through a pile of papers to find the one that was dunning her for a bill she forgot to pay.

Guiding her through a meditation? Ben felt ignored and he started to fume. There is nothing wrong with relaxing, but does it have to be disguised in some faux-mystical, oriental formula for reaching the no-state of no-thingness?

"You are now moving from the lustrous color orange to the heart *chakra* at the center of your being," Soji's clear, soft voice wafted through the room.

Irritated, Ben looked at his watch. His mother knew that he was on a tight schedule every Sunday and she was only on the *heart chakra?* That was in the middle of the body. How many more of those damn things were there?

"Feel your inner harmony and the luminous rays of celestial light emanating from your third eye,"

Ben was getting angrier by the minute. Soji knew he was there. She was purposely tormenting him. This sadistic tease could go on forever. *Sorry, I don't play those games.* Ben decided he would leave, but he couldn't go without letting his mother know he had been there. He reviewed his schedule for the day. Totally booked, but like a good son he had set aside an hour to spend with his mother. If she's busy, fine, but he couldn't rearrange his life to accommodate her every whim.

"Third eye?" Ben said aloud. "The last time I checked, mom had only two," He tried to make it sound like a joke. It wasn't received that way.

Bertha's eyes popped open. "Bennele, I didn't hear you come in." She picked herself up, but not without some considerable difficulty.

That was the first time Ben noticed how bad the osteoporosis in his mother's back had gotten.

"Was that supposed to be funny?" Soji was not laughing.

"We started your brunch but then we got distracted somehow," Bertha said as she hobbled into the kitchen, favoring one side. "I told Sonia about the pain I get in my back and she said she knew how to help me. We were marinating when you came in. It felt so good, like a nice nap. I don't sleep so good anymore. Anyway, I'll finish your brunch in no time, Sweetheart," she said as she entered the kitchen.

"Don't let me interfere, Mom," Ben said, suddenly ashamed. "I'm really glad Soji is helping you with your back. Please continue. It's just that I'm running late this morning. I can pick up something at the deli."

"God forbid!" she called out from the kitchen. "Pick up something at the deli? They charge you an arm and a leg, those bandits. Besides, Sunday is our day, Bennele. I look forward to it all week. I should miss out because of a little backache? Only when they put me in my grave, not before."

Bertha was already banging pots and pans as Soji got up from the floor. "Let me help you, Mom," Soji called out.

"No, darling, rest. It's almost ready. All I have to do is heat up the coffee and make eggs the way Benny likes."

Soji looked at Ben for a long moment.

"I really am sorry," Ben said "but I didn't know you were going to be busy this morning. If I did, I would have cancelled. I've got so many . . ." While he was talking, Soji turned away and walked to the kitchen. Ben flopped down on the couch, took out the draft of a speech he was working on and tried to concentrate.

"How do *you* like *your* eggs, Mom?" Soji said loud enough for Ben to hear.

"Me? I like everything," Bertha said. She could see where the question was going and deflected it.

"What about that, Ben?" Soji came into the living room.

"You know your mother. Does she really have no preferences at all, except for what she thinks will please you?"

"I honestly don't know, but I'd be deliriously happy if she made something *she* liked. I just don't want to spend the whole day talking about it," Ben pleaded. "Whatever she makes is fine. Believe me, I won't go away hungry. There are always bagels and blintzes in the freezer."

"Do you like I should defrost some strawberry blintzes?" Bertha called out from the kitchen.

"Sure, anything!" *Please don't engage me for the next ten minutes so I can stop feeling like an insensitive* putz *and proofread my damn speech.*

"Okay, Bennele. Strawberry blintzes coming up . . . Oh, my God!" Bertha shrieked.

"What's wrong?" Soji and Ben called out and ran into the kitchen together.

Bertha stood next to the open freezer compartment holding a baggie. "The blintzes are all moldy. I must have left the door open. What a stupid I am." She looked at Ben in utter desolation. "I can run out to the kosher market on the corner and get some fresh . . ."

"Please don't bother, mom," he said. "Eggs are fine."

Soji put her arm around Bertha and gently rubbed her bent back. Ben felt miserable. The tranquility he saw in her face when she was "marinating" cross-legged on the floor had totally disappeared.

"I feel so bad," Bertha agonized. "I know how much you like my strawberry blintzes and I ruined it for you, Benny."

"It's not a problem Mom, believe me. It's fine," Ben said and kissed her on the forehead.

"Five minutes, that's all it will take. Please, Bennele, I can get you . . ."

"What I really need now are a few minutes to look over my speech. Please believe me, Mom; eggs are perfectly fine. What would really help me is if we could please talk about it later while we eat."

Completely forlorn, Bertha took some eggs out of the refrigerator. Ben returned to his notes, avoiding the look Soji was giving him.

A few minutes later, she came into the living room and sat down next to Ben. She looked towards the kitchen. "Can Bertha hear us?" she asked in a low tone.

"I doubt it," Ben said softly. "Her left eardrum is pierced and she doesn't hear too well in the right one. Soji, I want you to know how sorry I am about disrupting your meditation . . ."

Soji abruptly cut him off. "I need to talk to you," she said icily.

"I'd like to talk to you, too, but I just don't have time this morning. Can we chat later?"

"I'm going to talk right now," Soji said. "I don't observe your rules."

"Okay." Did Ben have a choice?

"You have to explain something to me. How can you not answer your mother when she asks you a question? How can you not listen to her when she talks to you? Aside from being rude, doesn't that violate one of the Ten Commandments?"

"If you're suggesting that I don't honor my mother, neither she nor I would agree with you. She's never once complained . . ."

"How insensitive are you, Ben? Your mother would never complain to you, no matter how much pain or humiliation you caused her. You're her sun in the morning and her stars at night. *She* would never confront you about your appalling behavior, but that doesn't mean *I* won't."

"Appalling? There's nothing I wouldn't do for my mother.

I talk to her every day! I see her every week. I take her to every Yiddish or Russian show that comes to town and believe me, that's not how I prefer to spend my rare free evenings. Whenever I go to a restaurant I think she'd like, especially if there's music where she can get up and dance, I always . . ."

"You do lots of nice things for her, Ben. That's not what I'm talking about. She's alone all week and when she sees you on Sunday, she wants to talk. That's only natural. That's human. You don't say more than two words to her so rather than sit in silence she tries to talk to you but you won't let her. That's not only unnatural, it's inhuman."

"She talks all the time," Ben said, trying to keep his voice down as he felt his hackles rise. "I know she's capable of talking about important things occasionally, but most of the time the point is woven into some Byzantine labyrinth of trivia so convoluted that I don't know when to listen."

"So you shut her up."

"I call her every day and she can talk her heart out."

"You call her? You dial the phone and as soon as she picks up, you probably read a magazine or watch TV. Do you think she doesn't know what you're doing?"

"My mother is a very smart woman, Soji. I wouldn't be at all surprised that she knows what I'm doing and why, but I also know that's okay with her."

"How do you know that? She puts up with your crap but you have no idea what your mother thinks or feels or what *she* really wants."

"I certainly do. She wants me to get married, raise a family, be successful . . ."

"You're not listening, Ben. I'm not asking if you know what she wants for you, or for your brother and his kids, or for your father when he was alive, or for her "nice" neighbors. Think about her, just *her* for a moment, Ben. Do you have any idea what *she* wants for *herself?"*

What does my mother want for herself? The question spun around in Ben's head. *For herself?* He couldn't remember ever hearing his mother say that she wanted anything for herself. What could she possibly want that she wouldn't share with him—and why didn't he ever ask himself that question?

Ben suddenly flashed back to the year his father lost his bread business. Ben was in grade school, the steel workers at the mill were on a long strike and nobody had money. Families would come to his dad's bakery and beg for bread, but they had no money to pay for it. It broke his father's heart to see kids go hungry, so he gave them whatever he had and put it on a tab he knew would never be paid. Within a couple of months, he ran out of flour and had no money to buy more and had to shut down his bakery. Ultimately, he found a job with a baker who had prospered during those tough times by gouging the poor. But for nearly a year before his father found that job, Ben's family had to subsist on whatever his dad could do to bring home a dollar, whether it was delivering coal in the winter, ice in the summer or hauling junk. During those months, Bertha made the most delicious meals seemingly out of thin air. She worked hard to keep everyone's spirits high and every Sunday after Hebrew School, she brought home an ice cream "cake" the size of a small cookie. It was so tiny she was barely able to cut it into three pieces, one for dad, one for his brother Art and one for him. Bertha said she didn't like ice cream, so it worked out fine for everyone.

When Sol got a full-time job at Toasty-Taste bakery, they celebrated by going to the ice cream parlor where they all ordered large chocolate sundaes, not only his father, his brother and him, but his mother, too.

"I thought you didn't like ice cream." Ben remembered saying.

"I didn't used to," Bertha said. "I guess I developed a taste."

It was crushing to recall all those years of sacrifice coupled with Ben's ingratitude. Soji watched him without saying a word. Then, she put her hand on his and held it. Her presence was comforting, but the moment passed when Bertha dropped a pot in the kitchen and muttered, "Darn, I'm so clumsy!"

Soji jumped up to help Bertha, but Ben stopped her. "Soji, I have to ask you, how it is that you and my mother formed such a strong bond so quickly? I mean, you're as different as two people can be."

"You think I have some ulterior motive, like getting to the single rabbi through his mother?"

"That's ridiculous," Ben lied.

"There's nothing ulterior about it," Soji said. "You remember I told you where my name came from? What I didn't tell you was that martinets, not parents, raised me. For unrepentant communists, motherly love was bourgeois. I was suckled on party-line propaganda. What I wanted from my mother was love. All I got were lectures. At boarding school, my friends got letters from home talking about the family, the neighborhood, advice about dating and boys, affectionate birthday cards, reassurance when a friend was mean or a class was hard. My mother's letters were marching orders to rise up against the fascist imperialist corporate bosses and fight for the rights of the oppressed workers.

"When I first met Bertha at the Extravaganza in Vegas, we talked a little, exchanged some niceties. Then, somehow, I'm still not sure how it happened, I found myself pouring my guts out to her. I thought she would run away from me as fast as her little legs could carry her. She didn't. I shook my fists and bellowed. I must have looked like some nut going through primal scream therapy. When I finished, she took my hands in hers and looked into my eyes and said, 'I understand, dear. Believe me, I know from heartache. I see the anger in your eyes but I know that comes from deep wounds inside. Talk to me, angel, let me help you.' I fell into her arms and sobbed and she held me tight.

"In her embrace, I realized what I had hungered for all my life: A mother to listen to me and love me. Someone to let me cry or laugh or dream out loud. I was a mess. We cried and talked, and laughed, and talked and talked. No one had ever expressed such genuine interest in me, just me, not to make me do yet another soul-eroding movie, not to try to use me or influence me. This woman just wanted me to know that I was worth being listened to and, yes, loved.

"Then she asked me the sixty-four thousand dollar question. 'Tell me, sweetheart, deep in your heart, what do *you* really want?'

"What I really wanted," Soji's lips were clenched, "was my childhood. It was stolen from me and I want it back! It was hard to believe she could understand what I meant but she did and she held me while I bawled my heart out. I've had occasion to scream and howl in my life, but this went way beyond any of that. It was uncontrollable. There were all kinds of people around and Bertha, who is a fraction of my size, half-carried me to the ladies room and let me sob until I was all blubbered out. I don't know what it was, Ben, but there was something in her, a radiance, a simplicity, a purity that touched my very core. I knew that I needed this woman in my life. And the most miraculous part of it was that she felt the same way about me. As I've come to know her better, I love her even more. You look out for her most of the time, but when you falter I am going to be there for her."

"It's almost one o'clock, Benny." Bertha came running out of the kitchen and Ben could see that tears were shining in her eyes. She must have been listening. "What time do you have to give your speech?" she asked.

Ben looked at his watch. "Whoa! The event starts in about forty-five minutes. Fortunately, I don't go on for another hour, at least. Maybe even two."

"Come darling," Bertha said. "Everything's on the table. Better eat so you'll have strength to talk."

"Where are you speaking?" Soji asked.

"Saint Sophia, the glass cathedral on Sepulveda. It's an interfaith service. I'm delivering the keynote address, but every other clergyman in West Los Angeles will be 'saying a few words' so it may be a very long, drawn-out affair. I'd ask you to drop by but I'm sure it would bore the daylights out of you," Ben said, half-wishing Soji could hear him speak. Maybe she would see that he is not just an insensitive, unappreciative son. Maybe she would even forgive him—maybe even like him.

ABOUT AN HOUR into the interfaith meeting, Ben was finally called upon to deliver the address. The audience was fidgeting from all the pompous invocations and benedictions and people were looking at their watches as he stepped up to the podium.

As Ben looked out at the huge crowd, he was surprised to see his mother and Soji enter from the main entrance at the rear of the nave. Soji apparently wanted to sit in the back of the church but Bertha dragged her to the first row, where she sat and waved to her handsome son. Ben waited for them to get comfortable.

"Hi Mom," Ben said aloud, knowing how much pleasure that kind of recognition gave her. Soji seemed overjoyed to see Bertha *kvell*. As Ben watched them holding hands, something came over him. In a split second, he decided to chuck the speech he had prepared and looked around the lectern until he spotted a Bible. Ben turned to a familiar chapter and read aloud. "Whither thou goest, I shall go and whither thou lodgest, there I too will lodge . . . and where you die, there will I be buried . . ."

It took Ben a moment or two to organize his thoughts, then, it flowed. "The Book of Ruth is a powerful testament to love and loyalty, to friendship and devotion to one another. It's about two amazing women and how they turned each other's grief into triumph and misery into redemption." Ben told the biblical story faithfully, but the subtext was about Bertha and Soji. There could be no doubt in their minds that he was talking directly to them. Ben was asking his mother for forgiveness and thanking Soji for opening his heart.

After the service, Soji was waiting for Bertha outside the ladies room when he caught up with her. "You did good, Ben," she said.

"Intellectual, respectable or dignified?"

"You bordered on gorgeous." Soji's eyes were still red.

"Soji, I have to ask you. What *does* Mom want for herself? You're the only one who knows her that well."

"The one thing in this world beside her sons that could make Bertha happy and totally fulfilled would be to become a naturalized American citizen," Soji said. "Did you know that she includes America in her prayers every night along with you and your brother, Art and his kids"

"Yes. I did know that." Ben had been aware of his mother's fondness for America, but strangely, or perhaps true to form, he never gave it much thought. "I did hear stories about how hard life was in Russia and how much she loves America."

"What did you hear?"

"I heard that her mother died when she was an infant so her father raised her and her sister, Fayge. When he died, the two young girls travelled across Europe to get onto a ship to America."

"My God!" Soji said. " All your mother told you was that her father died? She didn't tell you that she and Fayge saw their father dragged out of their house and murdered right in front of them during one of the worst pogroms in Russian history?"

Ben felt the blood drain from his face. "No she didn't. I don't think she told Art this either. Maybe she was trying to protect us. When did it happen?"

"She was twelve or maybe fourteen. She said she wasn't sure because, 'who knew from birth certificates in Russia?' She and her sister fled to a nearby village where a Jewish family who survived the massacre took them in. They found a way to notify their Uncle Mechel, a widower who lived in Cleveland. He could arrange passage to America if the girls could get to Odessa. So Bertha and Fayge walked from village to village across Russia looking for the Jews of each town to provide shelter for the night. They did this over and over until they reached their ship in Odessa. After days in steerage they arrived in America where their Uncle Mechel took them in and raised them. Didn't Bertha ever tell you why she loves America so much?"

Ben shook his head.

"In Russia, as Bertha tells it, after the snow melted the unpaved streets would get all muddy. If a person fell down in the filth, the peasants would stand around and laugh. In America, if a person falls down in the street, everybody rushes to help them up. That's what America means to Bertha."

IF BECOMING A NATURALIZED CITIZEN was what Bertha wanted, Ben promised Soji he would do everything he possibly could to help her. Soji had a plan. The best thing Ben could do was to build Bertha's confidence and she would do the rest. A few days later, Ernie Fryberg put Soji in touch with a friendly immigration judge whose campaign he had financed. When Bertha was ready, Ernie would arrange a private session with the judge that was to include a quiz, followed by a swearing-in ceremony in the judge's private chambers at the Immigration Court in downtown L.A.

BERTHA WAS A NERVOUS WRECK. Soji and Ben tried to alleviate her anxieties but she worried anyway. It is fair to say that she spent most of her life worrying, even about the most insignificant things, so agonizing about a test that could enable her to realize the dream of a lifetime was understandable. Bertha insisted on studying for the quiz all day, every day. Soji was in Las Vegas during the week but they talked at length every evening. On weekends she spent endless hours helping Bertha study, trying to allay her fears by giving her positive reinforcement every time she got something right.

As it turned out, Bertha had learned a great deal. Memorizing dates wasn't her strong suit, but she accurately connected names with events, even though she altered them slightly. Her contextual arrangement turned out to be a valid system of mnemonics. Theodore Roosevelt became Theda

Roosevelt because she had a friend at May's department store in lingerie named Theda who also had bad handwriting like the "rough writers." The federalist papers became the "federation papers" because she and Ben's dad always contributed to the Jewish Federation, which collected money for the poor—and what could be more important than that?

Ben was amazed and impressed by Soji's patience. When she quizzed Bertha about Abraham Lincoln, his mother would go into a story about how her father's name was Abraham and he was killed when she was just a child . . . *If that were me, Ben thought, I'd have gone bonkers with all that rambling, but Soji patiently listened and when Bertha finished free-associating, Soji brought her back to the question.*

The Sunday before her interview, Ben quizzed his mother to see how well prepared she was. She must have been really nervous because she let Soji and Ben make brunch. She had never done that before. Ben knew how much passing the test meant to his mother and wanted nothing more than to help her pass with flying colors. After they cleared the table, Soji asked questions at random from the *Citizenship and Naturalization Manual.* Ben was astonished to see how much information Bertha had committed to memory. Louisiana Purchase? She knew the answer but couldn't understand why anybody would name their state "Lousy-Anna." The ship on which Francis Scott Key wrote the Star Spangled Banner? She knew everything except what was meant by the "rockets red clay." Bertha was as ready as she would ever be.

Downtown Los Angeles is a bizarre architectural mélange of New York's Fifth Avenue and Tijuana. When they arrived at the Immigration Court, they were ushered into the plush chambers of Judge Enrico Hernandez, an aristocratic-looking man with a mane of white hair and an avuncular demeanor. The judge patiently looked through a file on his desk, and then turned to Soji. "I see we have friends in common." Soji nodded.

He took an official-looking document out of the file and looked at Bertha over his pince-nez. "Mrs. Zelig, welcome to my chambers."

"Thank you judge, I can tell already you're a nice person. Maybe Your Honor will give me the pleasure of stopping by my house sometime so I can repay your hospitality with some strawberry blintzes. I just bought fresh."

Caught by surprise, Judge Hernandez let out a chortle. "That's the best offer I've received all day. I will definitely do that." It took him a moment to stop smiling.

"Now, Mrs. Zelig," he postured, "I understand you desire to become a naturalized citizen. Is that correct?"

"Yes it is, Your Honor."

"May I ask you a few questions?"

"It would be my honor, Your Honor," Bertha was nervous but ready.

He held up the *Citizenship and Naturalization Manual* and said, "I trust you've studied this?"

"I have. I did."

"And you know the answers to all the questions at the end of the pamphlet?"

"You bet your boots, Your Honor."

Judge Hernandez perused the pamphlet and read: "What do we call the first ten amendments to the constitution?"

"That's easy, Your Honor, The Bill of Rights." Bertha smiled and squared her shoulders.

"Can you tell me what two of those rights are?"

Ben tried to recall his high school civics class, but drew a blank and suddenly worried that Bertha would, too.

She didn't. "Speech and religion," Bertha answered proudly. "Very good. Now . . ."

"There's more, Your Honor. There's also assembly and press and . . ."

"Let's move on," the Judge said and closed his manual.

"I'm not in a hurry, Your Honor. Ask me some more questions. I studied up a lot more."

"I'm sure you have." The judge looked at the application forms on his desk. "I see you've filled out all the appropriate papers. This is all very good." Smiling, he said, "Mrs. Zelig, you have demonstrated to my satisfaction that you are ready to be sworn in."

Bertha turned pale. She turned to Soji. "Who is swearing? I never swear! What is the judge is talking about?"

"It's okay, Mom," Soji said. "Relax, you passed the test. There's nothing to worry about." Bertha gave an almost imperceptible nod.

Judge Hernandez took off his glasses and said in an authoritative, but gentle, voice, "Mrs. Zelig, would you please stand and raise your right hand."

Bertha stood and raised her shaking hand.

"Mrs. Bertha Criden Zelig, you have requested that the government bestow upon you its highest honor, that of citizenship in our great republic. Is that correct?"

Her hand trembled as she replied, "Republic? Uh . . . the first Republican president was Abraham Lincoln."

"Correct," he said. "One last question."

"Mrs. Zelig, do you plan to overthrow the government of the United States by force, violence or subversion?"

Silence. Bertha's right hand was now shaking uncontrollably. Thinking she didn't hear, Judge Hernandez tried again, more slowly. "Mrs. Zelig, I asked if you plan to overthrow the government of the United States by force, violence or subversion?"

Trembling, Bertha said softly, "I think—violence."

Soji and Ben were stunned.

Judge Hernandez, who was experienced in keeping witnesses on track, said, "What you really meant to say was none of the above, isn't that right, Mrs. Zelig?"

"I'm not sure, Your Honor," Bertha hesitated.

Soji and Ben shouted in unison, "JUST SAY NONE OF THE ABOVE!"

Bertha got the message. "You're absolutely right, Your Honor," she said. "None from above."

JUDGE HERNANDEZ said in all his years on the bench he had never before kissed anyone after the swearing in ritual but he couldn't resist Bertha. Nor could he resist her strawberry blintzes. Bertha was thrilled that the Judge agreed to come to her house for brunch with Soji and Ben, and she was beside herself watching the official representative of the United States of America enjoying her blintzes. She couldn't restrain her delight. "Look how nice the judge eats," she told Ben. "Why don't you ever have seconds when I make blintzes the way you like?"

"I just did, Mom."

"Never mind, there's plenty more."

After the Judge left, Bertha wrapped the remaining blintzes in saran wrap, then aluminum foil and, finally, zip-top baggies before stuffing them into her packed freezer.

Soji cleared the dishes while Ben helped his mom empty a large box of family photographs onto the dining room table.

Somewhere in that pile, Bertha hoped to find a suitable frame for her Certificate of Citizenship. She didn't find any so she went to the bedroom closet to look for more frames.

Ben remained at the table, perusing the snapshots. He was amazed to see how much his brother's kids had grown. When was the last time he saw them? He couldn't remember. Suddenly, Ben felt a hand on his thigh. He wasn't even aware that Soji had sat down next to him. She squeezed gently. A delicious tremor shot through Ben's body and he felt his heart beat faster.

"*Mazel tov*," she said.

"What for?"

"On the occasion of your *bar mitzvah*, Ben. Congratulations, today you became a man."

How Ben ached for her at that moment. Everything turned soft and hazy but he wasn't sure how to respond. Did she want him to kiss her? Would that offend her? Would it disrupt the moment? While Ben was trying to figure out what to do, she leaned in and kissed him full on the mouth. Her sweet fragrance dazzled Ben's senses and he thought his head was going to burst. She kissed him again. Wafting in space, he kissed her back. Ben had no idea how much time passed before he looked across the table. Bertha sat with her certificate in a gold frame watching him and Soji. Ben suddenly felt embarrassed. When he finally engaged his mother's eyes, she smiled sweetly.

Bertha turned from Ben to Soji and did something he had never seen his mother do before. She winked.

blood

2007.

"WHY PITTSBURGH?" Ben grumbled as they turned off the busy freeway and followed the directions to LAX. "Steel mills, soot—it's the ugliest city in the country. And they have snow. You'll hate it."

"Dad," Lizzy said patiently, "the steel mills are long gone. Besides, the place is teeming with culture. There are libraries, the ballet, museums and theaters. There's a Hillel on campus. And I've got a coat."

Ben shrugged. "But Pittsburgh . . . Why so far away?"

"Because Carnegie Mellon is the best drama school in the country and they picked me. Sutton Foster, my idol, went to

Carnegie Mellon. How many people do we know who were even accepted, let alone received a full scholarship?"

"Of course they want you. You're the best actress in America! Who is this Sutton Foster?"

"We saw her at the La Jolla Playhouse in *Thoroughly Modern Millie.*"

How could Ben forget that? It was his daughter's first professional musical and she was smitten with both the art form and the charming star.

"You know which show I like best. He tried to raise his voice several octaves. "I used to be a *schleppa* . . ."

"Now I'm Miss Mazeppa . . ." Lizzy continued. They both laughed.

"You were fantastic. I saw *Gypsy* every night The Players Club ran it. You're the best, Lizzy. I mean it. Mommy would have said, 'Now there's a REAL actress.'"

"No, Dad. Mommy would have said, 'Now, there's a REAL ACTOR.'"

Dan gave Lizzy a half smile.

As they waited in traffic to get up to the doors of the Delta terminal, Ben studied the perfect oval of his daughter's face, and for a second he swore he saw Soji looking back at him. He turned away before Lizzy could see his eyes tear up.

FIVE YEARS LATER it was still impossible to think about Soji without getting emotional. *I still get up every morning thinking she's here.* Who knew that the bat mitzvah would be the last of Lizzy's milestones Soji would ever see? It was such a glorious day. Ben had presided over countless *b'nai mitzvah*, but Lizzy outshone them all. Her lilting alto in the melodies, her flawless Hebrew and that speech she wrote, entirely without their help—it brought down the house! Her *tzedakah* project was so ambitious—raising donations and filling 100 backpacks for foster children—and yet she pulled it off with big-hearted devotion and a kind of business savvy that would have made his Uncle Joe proud. Soji's beautiful face had been radiant with the same pride and joy he felt. And then, two weeks later, she was gone. If only he hadn't agreed on that trip to the Caribbean.

There were a hundred other ways for us to celebrate our brilliant daughter. Why that cruise? It was going to be a family adventure, sail to the islands where they would explore hidden coves and secret beaches. Instead, Soji developed pneumonia shortly after they embarked. The hospital on St. Thomas assured them that with an IV full of antibiotics and some rest and she'd be just fine. The rest was a blur. One minute the doctor was trying to explain what "septic shock" meant and the next she was gone. Young, healthy and beautiful with everything to live for—and the Almighty had the audacity to take her. It all happened so fast; Ben couldn't absorb it for the longest time.

BEN IGNORED THE HONKS of the car behind him as he took Lizzy's luggage out of the trunk. He'd be damned if anyone was going to rush the goodbye to his daughter. After Soji's death they had clung to each other like survivors on a life raft. Eventually, they found their way back to dry land together and made a life. His favorite was the shows. He loved being a Drama Society parent volunteer and selling at the theater's concession stand or taxiing a carload of rowdy teenagers. It kept him alive. She kept him alive. And now she was leaving.

———

BEN KNEW HE SHOULDN'T bring it up again. "I just wish . . . You know, USC has a great film school and you could live at home."

Lizzy gently put her hand on her father's cheek. "We talked about this, Dad."

Ben picked up the handle of Lizzy's suitcase and started rolling it toward the terminal. He didn't want to nag, but he couldn't help it. "You'll call every day, right? Use the new cell phone. I bought you a plan."

"Of course I'll call. And Dad?"

"Yes, Lizzy?"

"Remember its Aliza from here on, just like we agreed." Ben nodded, too choked to speak.

She studied his face intently. "Thanks for everything, Dad. I love you."

Ben scrubbed a tear from his eye. "I love you, *ketzeleh*."

Aliza put her free hand in her father's and they continued silently into the terminal.

ON HIS WAY HOME, Ben ran into heavy traffic. At one point the 405 freeway was completely backed up so he took the first off-ramp. As he drove north on six-lane Sepulveda Boulevard, he found himself across the street from Hillside Memorial Park where Soji and Ben's mother, Bertha, were buried.

Without thinking, he drove in through the familiar gate and up the narrow road to the gravesites, surrounded on all sides by cypress trees, large oaks and thick yews. The terrain was so familiar, Ben believed he could find it blindfolded. The path to Bertha's gravesite was exactly twelve paces down the hill from

Soji's and his. They had bought adjoining plots when Bertha died. A small conifer provided just enough shade for the stone bench where Ben often sat when he came to visit his beloved.

He thought about the day Lizzy—*Aliza*—was born. It felt like his face would crack in half he was smiling so hard. He never saw Soji look more beautiful and he could have sworn there was a light shining from the baby's face. They needed an A to name her for Art, and it came to him in a breathless rush: "She's Aliza!" The name was Hebrew for joy. But now his joy was gone.

Was that why he was there now? Feeling weak, he sat on the stone bench, looking at the empty plot alongside Soji that waited for him. *Why not now, God?*

SOMETIME LATER, Ben stood up, went to his mother's grave, put on his *yarmulke* and recited the *Kaddish* and *El Maleh* prayers from memory. He slowly walked the twelve paces back to Soji's grave. He stood there and tried to recite the *Kaddish*, but nothing came out. He found himself unable to utter a single word, his throat painfully constricted. Finally, he pulled the *yarmulke* off his head and threw it on the ground.

When he arrived home, he was totally spent. Without thinking, he went to the kitchen, filled his glass with the Jack Daniels he kept on a high shelf out of parental habit, and took a few sips. He never did that this early in the day. A nightcap, sure. That sometimes helped him sleep. But in the afternoon?

He walked down the hall, past the gallery he had created—their family trip to Israel, Lizzy's graduation, the painting a congregant did of his late mother, Art's military citation, he and Uncle Joe in front of his first new car, and the silver framed wedding portrait of Soji—and went into his study. On his desk he saw the blinking light on his answering machine and pushed "messages."

"Hi, Rabbi." His secretary's voice was the last thing he wanted to hear. "Everybody's clamoring for you. You missed the Men's Club breakfast and Arnie Schwartz wants to know if you wouldn't mind . . ." Ben clicked "erase."

"Hello, Rabbi. Shirley Pearlstein here. Jake's going in for gall bladder surgery this afternoon and he wants to you to come by and . . ." Ben clicked "erase."

"Rabbi Zelig, this is Jack Warburg. I'd like to talk to you about making a contribution of some of my paintings in exchange . . ." Ben clicked "erase" and, rather than listen to any other messages, he erased them all.

He went into the kitchen again and was surprised to see that his glass of J.D. was empty. He refilled it and walked back to his study, but stopped this time in front of Soji's picture. He turned on the hall light so he could see her better and felt the floodwaters overtake him. An unearthly howl escaped his lips. He brought his face close to his radiant bride then took a surprised step back. He looked again at the reflective glass over the portrait, but saw . . . *nothing*. His image was not reflected. The master lights in the living room were on. Why was he not visible in the glass?

He was still standing there perplexed when he heard a soft wailing sound outside his front door. He opened it and looked around. Not a soul. He followed the sound and finally, he saw it. The *mezuzah* on his door post was loosely dangling from one nail as if struggling to free itself. The wailing sounds became louder. Unthinking, Ben went into the kitchen and came out with a hammer. He opened his front door wide and digging in the clawed end, tore out the *mezuzah*, and threw it as hard as he could into the air. The wailing sound stopped just as the phone began to ring and ring. When Ben picked it up, a man's voice said "I'm looking for Rabbi Zelig . . ."

"So am I," Ben said and dropped the phone.

THE CONTENT OF THE BOTTLE of Jack Daniels was considerably lower when Ben staggered back into the kitchen and started the coffeemaker. He had to call Lizzy—*Aliza*—to make sure she had arrived safely and he couldn't do it in this state. It was going to be a strong pot—he lost count at five tablespoons of ground coffee—but what did it matter? He pushed "brew" and stumbled into the living room. He stopped in front of the large mirror above the *chaise longue.*

Nothing. Still no reflection. He put out a hand to steady himself on the side table and felt something. Looking down, he saw a framed document. It was his *S'micha,* the diploma he received at his ordination thirty years ago. Why was it in the living room and not on the wall of his study? Had he been looking at it?

He picked up the thick frame and read from the diploma in Hebrew: *Benjamin, son of Solomon Zelig, shall henceforth be called, Rabbi, Scholar, Teacher and Preacher in Israel,* It was signed by six world-renowned Jewish scholars.

Ben's hand trembled and the heavy, framed document fell and shattered on the hardwood floor. The sound of cracking glass reverberated through his brain. He picked up the suddenly free piece of parchment. The first name on his *S'micha* was Professor Jacob ben Moshe Rothstein. Professor Rothstein! His mentor, his personal guide all the years he studied at the Rabbinical Academy. Images of his beloved teacher raced through his brain.

He remembered introducing Rothstein to Soji. Ben wanted

her to see the Rabbinical Academy where his spiritual life had blossomed. He had butterflies when he knocked on the office door, but they quickly dispersed when the door flew open and he found himself in his mentor's embrace. Professor Rothstein then took Soji's hand and smiled. "My dear," he said, "your beauty is exceeded only by your wisdom in selecting this extraordinary man to be your husband."

Then there was the day he tried to drown himself in a New York City thunderstorm. He had just gotten the call from Art's wife, Marge, that his brother's F-14 Tomcat had disintegrated in midair and he was floundering up Broadway drenched to the skin, not really caring where he was going when he nearly crashed into someone. He looked up to see who it was and was drawn into the warm, dark gaze of Jacob Rothstein. The professor covered Ben with his umbrella, exposing himself to the torrential downpour and then embraced Ben with surprising strength with his free hand.

"I heard! I heard about your brother, of blessed memory, and I'm heartbroken," the professor shouted over the raging storm. Ben collapsed into tears and they stood together in the rain, weeping.

Inspired, Ben raced back to his study and looked at the graduation photo of himself with the professor, both in robes, the venerable rabbi's flowing white beard making him resemble an Old Testament prophet. Professor Rothstein, the one person in the world who could see beyond what was visible to most people. He learned more from Professor Rothstein's gestures, the look in his twinkling eyes, the way he lit his pipe as the match burned precariously close to his fingers, than from years of studying texts. Professor Rothstein had a way of smiling as he reflected on a problem that put even the most complex quandaries into a clear context that enabled Ben to grow from each encounter. He was the only person who could understand why Ben's faith, which had been driving force of his life, had deserted him.

Ben's eye fell on the *Tanakh*, the Hebrew Bible, on his desk sitting open to the Book of Job. Was he a latter-day Job? So many treasured people, only to lose them all in his later years, one by one, until he was a trembling shell. Uncle Joe, MaryAnne, Art, Mom and Soji, all taken by a terrible death. Now, his very reason to live was in Pittsburgh—and she was no longer his Lizzy! He wasn't ready to lose his baby forever to be replaced by the adult stranger she would become. He wailed in anguish as he knocked piles of books, papers, and correspondence onto the floor. "Am I supposed to continue to be a believer? In who? Believe in the God who took away everyone who gave meaning to my life?"

He hurled the *Siddur Sim Shalom*, his prayer book, and heard it crash against the far wall. "NO MORE! THERE IS NO JUDGE AND NO JUSTICE! I RENOUNCE YOU GOD!" he bellowed. Suddenly, he froze. Hearing the words of Alisha ben Abuya, the classic apostate, coming out of his mouth was so terrifying, he was struck dumb.

He couldn't think and sank to his knees. "Lizzy . . . Lizzy darling, I can't abandon you. I won't leave you . . . but how can I regain the will to go on?" he croaked. Who could he turn to? He looked again at the graduation photo, now hanging off kilter on the wall.

At six A.M. Los Angeles time, Ben placed a call to New York. "Professor Rothstein, this is Ben Zelig. Thank you for remembering. No, I'm afraid all is not well. I am thinking about coming to New York and it would mean a great deal to me if . . ."

"I SUBMITTED MY RESIGNATION to the Temple Board," Ben said, looking up at the familiar piles of books leaning out of the shelves in Professor Rothstein's office. They had embraced warmly when Ben arrived, but something was off. As long as he could busy himself preparing tea and serving cookies, Professor Rothstein was his usual charming self. But the moment Ben broached the subject that was eating him alive, his mentor sank into uncharacteristic silence. Ben watched as Professor Rothstein sipped his tea for a long moment then put down his cup.

"I see," Rothstein said absentmindedly.

Ben was surprised at the tepid response. Rabbi Rothstein knew about his losses and the lingering effect they had on him. Where was the illuminating insight to address Ben's dilemma and somehow convince him not to act precipitously? In the past, he might start with a Hasidic parable or literary allusion. This time, his beloved professor said nothing. Instead, he sat for a long time, staring into space.

"The board didn't accept my resignation," Ben said, thinking that Rothstein didn't understand the extent of his misery. "They asked me to take some time off and think about it, but I can barely think. Every time I close my eyes I see a funeral for someone I love. Art at Arlington. Mom and Soji at Hillside Memorial. And now my light, my Lizzy, is in Pittsburgh! I'm desperate."

Professor Rothstein said nothing. Ben tried to hide his surprise. They sat in silence until his mentor reached for his tea cup, raised it to his lips again and his hand began to shake. Ben took the cup and placed it on the table. A tear rolled down the old man's cheek into his flowing white beard and he bit his lip so as not to weep aloud.

Ben was stunned. *What have I done?* "Forgive me, Professor, I . . ."

"You have a serious problem, Ben," Professor Rothstein said.

"I know," Ben said, "but I never intended to upset you. I'm so sorry."

Professor Rothstein interrupted. "You have a problem, but so do I. A serious problem. A *very* serious problem."

It took Ben a moment to realize that his beloved professor was struggling with his own demons and his anguish had nothing to do with Ben.

After a brief silence, Professor Rothstein wiped his eyes. "More tea?" He rose from his chair and tried to lift the pot, but it shook in his hand. Ben took it from him and led him back to his chair.

"What is it, Rebbe?" Ben asked.

Professor Rothstein's face was ashen. "I can't trouble you with my . . ." more tears filled his eyes and he couldn't go on.

"Please talk to me, Rebbe," Ben pleaded. "You've been there for me all these years. Now you need help and I am here for you."

The old man stopped and stared at Ben. "You are here for me?" He studied Ben's face silently for a long time. "Are you the one?"

Ben didn't know what to say. Rothstein grabbed the lapels of Ben's sports jacket. "You! You are here for me!" Suddenly Rothstein smiled broadly and released Ben. "You have arrived!" He raised his hands to heaven: "Hallelujah!"

Ben froze in place while his beloved professor gazed into his eyes as though he were reading a crystal ball.

Professor Rothstein's face became radiant. He stood up, adjusted the *yarmulke* on his head, closed his eyes and sang aloud in Hebrew, "Lord, You alone have seen the anguish of my soul. You heard my call from the depths of despair. I thank Thee, Master of the Universe, for answering my prayer—and sending my deliverer!"

He grabbed Ben in a bear hug as tears of joy rolled down his cheeks. "You will find her and bring her back!" Professor Rothstein said. "You will return my sweet, pure child to me before it is too late because you are a bearer of the light, a messenger of the Holy One, blessed be He."

BEN WAS IN SHOCK, but it didn't fully register until he left Professor Rothstein's office. There was no point arguing that he was *not* sent on a divine mission, but rather had come to save his own life. How could he say "no" to someone who had been like a second father to him? And as a father himself the idea of being estranged from Lizzy was unspeakable. He couldn't allow his rebbe to suffer that kind of torment.

On a bench outside the Academy he produced his cell phone and reading glasses. He flipped the phone open and dialed. A cheerful voice came on the line. "You've reached the phone of the one and only Aliza B. Zelig. You know what to do!"

"Lizzy—Aliza—it's Daddy. I'm in New York visiting Professor Rothstein. Do you remember meeting him when you were little? Anyway, give me a call and let me know you got this. I miss . . ." Another beep cut off the rest of his message. He stifled an urge to throw the phone to the pavement and looked at the piece of paper his rebbe had given him. He punched in the number.

When a woman answered, he said "Naomi, you don't know me. My name is Ben Zelig. I'm a friend of your father's . . ."

"I have to put you on hold," the woman cut him off.

Ben waited for about five minutes. Just as he was about to hang up, she came back on the line. "Sorry. That was 911 and I had to take the call."

"911! Are you serious?"

"No, but since I don't know you I don't see why I should assign you any priorities."

"I'm a former student, friend and ardent admirer of your father. He . . ."

"How well do you know him?" She cut in again.

"He is the closest I have ever come to meeting a saint," Ben said.

"Really?" There was a silence. "That's not the word that comes to my mind when I think of him, which isn't often."

Ben wasn't sure how to continue the conversation. "What word would you choose?"

"Neglectful, selfish, insensitive to name but a few. Shall I go on?"

Under other circumstances Ben would have told her to go to hell and hung up, but he couldn't. What had Jacob Rothstein done to deserve this? Finally, Ben said, "I guess you're not very fond of your father."

"I hate the son of a bitch. Got to go, 911 is calling back," she said and the line went dead.

Ben called again. "Five minutes is all I'm asking. Just tell me where I can meet you and you can start counting the minute I arrive. Please, five minutes. I can't tell you how important it is."

There was a pause. "How bad is it? Is he dying or something?"

"Or something," Ben said. "Quickly, tell me where we can meet. I've got 911 on *my* other line now."

"You've got . . . ?" She chuckled and told Ben to meet her on the northeast corner of 125th street and Lexington Avenue.

"How will I recognize you?"

"I have big boobs and a small butt."

"Will you be covering them with clothes I might recognize?"

"Wear a black turtleneck. I'll recognize you."

"You think I'll be the only one wearing a black turtleneck?"

"I'm sure of it. Turtlenecks have been out for years. Only geeks and nerds still wear them. That includes rabbis, by the way."

"What time?"

"Six twenty-five. That will give you exactly five minutes before I start work."

"Can we make it earlier?"

"Why?"

"It's Friday evening and the Sabbath begins . . ."

"Screw you and screw the Sabbath," she said and hung up.

Ben dialed again. "This is 911 again. Please don't hang up."

"Give me one reason, five words or less."

"My cell's out of minutes," Ben said. "That's five words if you don't take off for the apostrophe."

"You sure you're a rabbi?"

"Why do you ask?"

"Because you don't sound like a complete nerd."

"My daughter would disagree. She would assure you I can be as big a nerd as anybody. How about six o'clock?"

"Eighteen-thirty-one Harlem River Drive, corner of 129th Street, apartment 6D." *Click.*

When Ben arrived he was surprised to see a row of historic

brownstones in various stages of renovation. The number she had given him was the one still dilapidated building on the block. It clearly had been subdivided many times by the number of names at the buzzer. Once pressed, the buzzer shrieked incessantly as did several voices cursing him out over the intercom. Fortunately, one of them took pity and the door opened. Ben prepared to climb the stairs when he heard commotion coming from the floors above him.

"You been cheatin' on me, you bitch," an angry man with a thick Puerto Rican accent screamed.

"No, I ain't neither," a woman cried. "I been true to you, baby."

The sound of a fist punching a face was followed by a loud "ow!" and someone went tumbling down a flight of stairs.

Before he could move, Ben heard the steps creaking. Were they coming his way?

"Don't lie to me, *puta*. I know what you been doin'. Admit it! You don't love me no more. Admit it or I'll kill you, bitch!" Another punch, another groan and another tumble down a flight of stairs.

Now the woman was really crying. "I swear to God I been true to you. I love you, baby, I ain't lyin'."

Ben couldn't stand by and do nothing while a woman was being beaten to death. He felt for his cell phone and started up the stairs. The wooden banister was broken but he held onto the wall until he touched something slimy, and then decided it was better to just walk slowly and maintain his balance. The sounds of the brutal beating filled the hallway. Ben couldn't understand why nobody else came out to stop the vicious assault and prepared to dial 911. When he reached the third story, he finally understood what was going on.

A very large black woman stood at the top of the third floor staircase as a small Puerto Rican man, bloody and bruised, climbed up to her from where he had obviously fallen. "You lousy *puta*! You hate me, don' you?" The little man said with blood dripping from his mouth. "Say it, you lyin' *bitch*. I want to hear it from you. Say it or I'll kill you." Now he was screaming in her face.

Tears streamed down her face as she pleaded. "Please believe me, baby. I always loved you. I always will." Then, she reached back and punched him in the face again. He groaned loudly as he fell back down the stairs. She wept as he slowly climbed back for more.

"You better quit lyin' or I'll . . ." he collapsed into her arms.

"Oh, baby!" the woman cried as they inexplicably started kissing passionately.

Ben climbed past the dueling lovers who didn't even acknowledge him. Out of breath, Ben finally reached the top floor where two tiny apartments straddled the stairwell and knocked on the door of apartment 6D. An attractive young woman with an hourglass figure and take-charge attitude opened the door. She wore a black sweater that emphasized her full bosom and black leggings that left no doubt about her small waist and firm bottom. Her auburn hair was pulled back into a tight ponytail.

"Naomi . . . ?" Ben tried to draw air.

"I have two questions," she said as she waited for him to catch his breath. "Are you alive and if so, are you Ben?"

"Yes . . . Ben Zelig. 911. Sorry," he wheezed.

"You're late."

"There was some commotion on the way up."

"Oh, yeah. Second Friday of the month. Denise and Pedro. When they get paid, they get drunk. When they get drunk, they fight."

"But she nearly killed him," Ben managed to gasp out.

Naomi shrugged. "This one seems to be harder to kill than the last one." As the pain in Ben's lungs receded, he quickly checked out the place. The interior was sparse but surprisingly tidy. A futon covered in what looked like Indian sari fabric, a vinyl loveseat that clearly had been rescued from the curb but had been cheerfully resurrected with multi-colored duct tape, and a large painting of a reclining nude with a likeness of its owner covering a broken window. As he looked around, Ben noticed a small table covered with paints and brushes and several more canvases in various stages.

"You paint?" he asked in surprise.

Naomi ignored him and slung her backpack over her shoulder. "I'm late for work. You can walk with me."

"HE MUST BE PRETTY SICK, HUH?" Naomi asked as she raced through heavy Harlem traffic. Her pace was that of a dancer and Ben had to practically run to keep up.

"Why do you say that?"

"I haven't spoken to my father in over five years and you're the first emissary he's sent. Why now? Why you?"

"We're both fathers of daughters and I wanted to help."

"I don't buy that."

"It's true."

"Sure. Try again."

"Your father has done so much for me over the years but never asked a thing from me until now. He said it was urgent that I see you immediately and that was good enough for me. I've come to question a great many things over the past years but one thing I know with absolute certainty. Your father has the insight of a prophet."

"You love him, don't you?"

"I worship him. To me, Jacob Rothstein is a saint, a second father. The most important thing in his life is disseminating kindness. I remember walking down West End Avenue one Shabbat afternoon when a woman staggered out of a bar. It was a bright day and seeing how she shielded her eyes from the sun, it was clear that she had been drinking for some time. The people around us snickered at her as she stumbled along the crowded street. Not your father. He smiled and extended his hand. He looked into her eyes with warmth and compassion. He told her she looked like a charming woman and he hoped she was enjoying the beautiful weather. The woman held onto his hand for the longest time. At first she seemed suspicious and tried to figure his angle, but soon the gentle look in his eyes relaxed her.

"'My hair could look a lot better,' she said, 'but I can't sit in a beauty parlor all day 'cause I got to go to work.' Your father assured her that her hair was fine and she looked lovely. I'll never forget the expression on her face when he said that. At first she blushed, then tears rolled down her cheek. He raised her hand to his lips and kissed it. When we left, she walked toward the subway, erect and proud. She didn't stumble or falter like a derelict, but joined the crowd, feeling like a person worthy of being on this planet."

"Are you capable of saying anything without delivering a sermon?" she sneered.

"I didn't mean to bore you, but I don't know if you've heard those stories about your father."

"All my life."

"And—you still hate him?"

"I used to love my father more than anyone in the world,

but he did the worst thing to me that a father can do to his daughter. He abandoned me."

Ben didn't know how much she would reveal, and, judging from the intensity of her tone, he wasn't sure he wanted to hear it. Still, he asked. "Do you want to tell me about it?"

"Are you asking as a psychiatrist, a rabbi, or just a nosey *schmuck*?"

"I'm not a psychiatrist," Ben said, "but that still leaves you with a couple of options."

She dismissed the notion with a wave of her hand. "He's not worth talking about, not even to a nosey *schmuck*. Naomi stopped at the entrance to a club with a blinking sign that read *All Girls! All Live! All Nude! All the Time!* "This is where I work," she said. He could hear the challenge in her voice.

This was worse than he could have imagined. Was his saintly rabbi's daughter a stripper? He thought of Lizzy and froze.

She opened the door and turned to Ben. "In or out?"

"Is this a joke?" Ben asked.

"Do I look like I'm joking?" Her voice was ice cold.

"But I want to talk to you," Ben pleaded.

"A lot of lonely nerds do, but they pay for it, even with my clothes on."

"That's not why I came to see you . . ."

She laughed. "I am playing with you now. I know everything I need to know about you but you don't have a clue about me. Come in, you might learn something."

What were his options? He had none, so he followed her. Inside the sleazy club, they were hit by a blast of music from two huge speakers flanking the stage. Naomi led the way to a table where a fat man with a few curly, greasy hairs stretched across a balding head, dined on a large plate of something orange and lumpy. Ben didn't get the gentleman's name but it was something like Chooch. Naomi introduced Ben as her rabbi.

Chooch looked from Ben to Naomi. "Delilah, you got a rabbi? A Jewish rabbi? No shit!"

"No shit," Naomi assured him.

Surprised, the fat man looked at Naomi and smiled broadly. "Whaddaya, some kinda Jew? I thought you was Puerto Rican. Hey, this is big. Half the *bakalas* that come in here are Jews. Why didn't you tell me this before? This is big!"

Naomi ignored him, turned on her heel and headed to the back of the theater. "Sit!" she barked at Ben pointing to at an empty table. He sat.

On stage was a dancer in stilettos, a G-string and not much else straddling a large pole. Ben turned his back on the stage as he miserably reviewed the last 12 hours. He had started the day with the razor-thin hope that somehow he could resolve the spiritual crisis that was strangling him. Instead, he was in a cesspool of depravity on an impossible mission, and the one person he had put his faith in deluded himself into thinking that Ben was the engine of *his* salvation!

Finally, the dancer teetered off the stage. A voice came over the loud speaker. "And now, let's give a big Harlem *shalom* to Delilah, Israel's secret weapon."

Ben had a sick feeling it was going to be Naomi. He tried to only take a brief glance, but couldn't move as she gracefully sauntered on stage wearing an army helmet, bandoliers, garters and the tiniest skirt he'd ever seen. Her eyes were rimmed with black and he caught a hint of gold glinting from the center of her G-string.

As she shed the bandoliers and the ridiculous excuse for a skirt, drunken men tried to stuff dollar bills into her garter. Ben couldn't help but believe that her soul was in torment as she straddled the pole and gyrated lasciviously, naked except for her G-string—and on the Holy Sabbath, no less. Was he kidding himself that sitting in this cesspool trying to reason with this angry, foul-mouthed young woman was going to restore his faith? Was it really worth violating the Sabbath? And did he still care?

FINALLY, NAOMI CAME OUT FRONT, dressed simply in jeans and a sweater, her backpack slung over her shoulder, still in makeup. "I'm out of here," she said, barely slowing down as she passed Ben's table.

"Where are you going?" Ben asked.

"To my next gig." She picked up the pace as they raced down 125th Street.

"Why do you do this?"

"Why? I like eating, having a place to live, why do you think, shit-head?"

"But humiliating yourself . . ."

"You're the one who humiliates himself. You make a living by mumbling nonsense words to people who don't understand them. I actually perform a service."

"By stripping?"

"That's not all I do." She was moving even faster now. Dan was barely able to keep up. Naomi stopped at a small brick building. There was a sign with an arrow that pointed down a flight of stairs: *Guide to the Perplexed Comedy Club*. Naomi headed down the stairs.

"Why are we here?" Ben asked peering over Naomi's head at a door painted with a garish cartoon that resembled *MAD* magazine's Alfred E. Neuman.

"I've got the seven P.M. timeslot tonight." Naomi pulled the door open and pointed to a dimly lit room. "You go that way. I go this way."

A tall, thin young man with a high fade hairstyle emerged out of the gloom. "You're on in five, Naomi. Who's this?"

"My agent. He's with me, Kareem."

Kareem studied Ben. "Agent, huh? Say something in agent."

"Uhh . . . *abi gezunt,*" Ben tried.

"If you say so. OK. Go ahead, Mr. Agent."

Ben took a seat in the darkest corner he could find, hoping that whatever Naomi was about to do it would include keeping her clothes on. He looked around. The room was small, there couldn't have been more than a dozen tiny tables and barely half of them were full. It occurred to Ben that this was a poor timeslot because most people were just heading to dinner. A scan of the audience confirmed that. A few tourists, maybe from the Midwest and Japan, and a sprinkling of younger people who seemed to be just waiting. He turned back to the tiny stage, which was really not much more than a raised platform. Suddenly, a small spotlight with a garish blue gel illuminated Kareem, who was standing at a microphone.

"Ladies and gentlemen, for our first set let's give a perplexed welcome to the one and only Naomi Darling!"

There was a smattering of polite applause as Naomi walked up to the mic. "How's everyone doing tonight? Anyone drunk yet?"

A man in the crowd shouted, "Not yet, but I'm working on it!"

"Let me know when you get there," Naomi retorted.

She unhooked the microphone from its stand and stepped toward the edge of the stage. "Raise your hand if your parents left you at a highway rest stop."

The rowdy raised his hand.

"And you've been drinking ever since, right?" The audience snickered.

Naomi continued. "I have the distinction of being left at rest stops in multiple countries and always by my father. It's especially fun if the rest stop is in Cairo. You should try it some time. Doesn't every little girl want to be at the center of an international incident because her father couldn't be bothered to remember where he left her?" There were some nervous giggles.

"Mom used to have to call him and say, 'Listen up! We've got a kid. Bringing her home alive and in one piece is not optional.'" There were some genuine laughs.

"Susan Storm of the Fantastic Four had nothing on me. I was the Invisible Girl. Well—invisible until someone famous came to visit. Have you ever had to do an impromptu solo recital for Beverly Sills? Daddy dearest said, 'Sing your favorite song, Naomi *bubbeleh.*'"

Naomi gave it a beat. "I don't think she was really into the Sex Pistols."

More laughs.

"Interesting childhood, right? One part, performing monkey; one part, Invisible Girl. And I haven't even gotten to the best part. My father wasn't just any self-indulgent asshole with his head in the clouds. No, he was a rabbi. And not just *a* rabbi. He was *the* rabbi. The chief *putz* at the New York Academy of Spiritual Putzhood.

"Who the hell raised me, you ask? Rabbi Chauncey Gardener. You remember him from the movie, *Being There*, don't you? Everyone thought he was a freaking genius but he couldn't wipe himself without help. That was my father. My old man—and I do mean old, he dated Queen Esther in high school—still thinks I'm an adorable child in pigtails and a plaid skirt. And he's right. That's what I take off five days a week at the strip club. All the daddies love it." There was scattered laughter.

Kareem reappeared. "Let's give a big hand to Naomi Darling," he said reaching for the microphone.

BEN WAS STANDING OUTSIDE the club trying to call Lizzy when Naomi reappeared, moving fast. With a sigh he snapped his phone shut and followed her at a near run. "Do you ever just walk?" he demanded.

"You're still here." She stepped into the crosswalk and weaved around oncoming pedestrians.

"Naomi, we have to talk. I'm concerned about your perception of your father."

"MY perception? What do you know? Anyone ever treat you like a pet lapdog? Just there to be dressed up and admired but heaven forbid you should have real needs. Tell me, Rabbi, your loving parents ever forget you existed and leave you somewhere?"

"You mean the rest stop joke was real?"

"Real? Ha! That was nothing. Your dear absent-minded professor was constantly forgetting he was supposed to be looking after me and would lock me out of the apartment or make me wait hours to be picked up or—best of all—forget I was being released from the hospital and needed to be taken home."

"The professor is a little forgetful, but I'm sure you exaggerate. I'm a father and let me tell you, no parent forgets his daughter is in the hospital."

"Oh really, Rabbi Know-it-All? Naomi barked out a harsh

laugh. "You think your precious rebbe and his band of idiot disciples share everything with you? Tell me, what happened to Steve Horowitz?"

"Never heard of him."

"Of course not. There's no record of him, but he was real enough to get me pregnant. Then—poof! No more baby and it was as if he never existed. "

"How old were you?"

"Seventeen. After Mama died I needed someone to love."

Ben started to put a hand on her shoulder but stopped. "I'm sorry about your mother. I wasn't able to come east for the funeral."

To his surprise, Naomi softened. "It's OK."

She seemed far away for a moment, and then snapped back. "No one would have noticed you. The entire world came. Dad was in his element. Why comfort your daughter when you can hug Harry Belafonte and Elie Weisel?" She turned on her heel and took off down the street. Ben followed at a trot.

"I don't doubt what you say, but I know your father loves you," Ben said.

"You know nothing," she said and walked toward the club where the neon screamed: *All Nude! All Girls! All live! All the time!*

"Naomi, I still don't understand why you feel the need to appear naked." Ben gave silent thanks that his relationship with Lizzy never brought him this sort of grief.

"God, you are dense beyond belief! Why do I strip in front of pathetic men? Have you not heard a word I said?" Disgusted, she pulled her backpack off her shoulder and walked toward the side door of the club.

Naomi opened the door and stopped. She stared at the ground intensely for a moment then looked Ben in the eye.

"You know, I really loved my father when I was little. I thought he was the greatest man in the world. Did he ever tell you I wanted to become a rabbi? Can you believe that?"

Ben's mouth dropped open at the revelation.

Naomi's voice softened. "Do yourself a favor and go home." The heavy metal door slammed behind her with a final *clang*.

Ben stood in front of the flashing neon lights for several minutes, trying to figure out what to do next. He walked back and forth down the block. If this was part of some cosmic plan, obviously, he wasn't following it very well. He thought about Lizzy and how, if he had been in the rebbe's place, his most fervent prayer would be for someone to rescue her from such a terrible fate. Resolved, he opened the door and went in.

The entrance way was dark except for intermittent flashes of light in the distance. The cacophonous sounds from inside were deafening. At the end of the corridor, there was a bouncer he hadn't seen earlier. Silhouetted by the swirling lights from the interior of the club, he looked like a psychedelic Mr. Clean.

"Ten dollars," he said.

Ben had never seen such a blank stare. The man's eyes didn't seem to be connected to anything. *So this is what a golem looks like*, Ben thought.

"Ten dollars," the man said again, louder.

"I don't carry money on the Sabbath," Ben stuttered. "I'm a rabbi and I'm here because I'm a friend of Naomi—that is, Delilah—well, not a friend, exactly . . ."

"No money? What you think this is, the Salvation Army? Get your skinny ass out of here!"

Ben opened his mouth to explain further, but realized that wasn't a smart idea. He left without a word.

He stood outside for several minutes wondering how to get past Mr. Clean when he decided to try the side door in the alley that Naomi had used. Halfway down, he saw two figures rolling a drunk. His heart thundering in his chest, he turned to leave, but blocking his path was Mr. Clean. He waited until Ben approached, then grabbed him, twisted him around and with one hand on Ben's neck and the other on the seat of his pants, flung him out of the alley.

Ben was slowly picking himself up, both knees throbbing, when Mr. Clean seized him again. He carried Ben by his collar and pants for half a block before throwing him another five or ten feet. For a fraction of a second Ben felt as though he was soaring in space, then he crashed onto the pavement. Even as the world spun around him he knew that he had better get as far away from his tormentor as his wounded legs would carry him. Lightheaded and out of breath, Ben pulled himself upright with the help of a lamppost. He staggered into the intersection to look at the street signs to see where he was but they were entirely covered with graffiti. Where could he be? This didn't look like any part of Harlem he recognized. All he was sure of was that he was hurting, the sun had set, and the Sabbath had descended.

A slight vibration in his coat shook him out of his reverie. Still standing in the middle of the street, he pulled out his phone and squinted at the screen: "Lizzy" it read.

Before Ben could open the phone he felt a violent shock down his back. The world tilted on its axis and then went dark.

HE DIDN'T KNOW HOW LONG he had been out when he opened his eyes, but he realized there was an unshaved man staring down at him. Behind the man was a taxi with the door open and the motor running. They were in the middle of the cross section.

"You're not dead? Watch where the hell you're going next time, jackass!" The man gave a final look of disgust, jumped back into the cab, slammed the door and drove off.

"Are you all right?" A well-dressed young couple looked down at him with concern. The man tucked a hand under his arm. "Do you think you can stand? Let me help you."

With excruciating slowness, Ben got to his feet.

"I think your phone got run over," said the young woman handing him the smashed appliance. "Are you sure you're all right?" the woman asked again.

"I don't think so," Ben croaked. Somehow they took that as a "yes."

"You better get out of traffic," the man said as he took the woman's arm and they crossed the street.

Ben fought a wave of vertigo. Flickering lights from the clubs, restaurants and theaters triggered violent contrasting flashes in his brain. His eyes twitched spasmodically. The light changed three or four times and Ben still wasn't sure whether or not it was safe to move.

"Make up your mind, man! Don't go blocking the whole street," an elegantly dressed lady behind him began to push him across the wide thoroughfare.

"Please help me, ma'am," he said. "I'm lost."

"Tell me something I *don't* know," she said when they reached the curb. Pointing to a street sign, she said, "Check the sign, fool."

Spray-painted words had been scrawled over the sign making it impossible to read the name of the street, but the graffiti was familiar. It said—faith. He looked again. FAITH! Ben heard himself babbling. "Faith? If I still had my faith, I wouldn't be here! RABBI ROTHSTEIN, HELP ME!"

An elderly Black man with a white beard, wearing a square

black *yarmulke*, stopped in front of Ben. "Did I hear you say Rabbi Rothstein? Would that be Rabbi Jacob Rothstein?"

"Yes, yes," Ben said. "He's my rabbi. Do you know him?"

"Of course, he's my rabbi, too," the old man smiled, extending his hand. "I'm Brother Abner Scarsdale, Sexton of Temple B'nai Sheba."

Ben shook his hand. "Zelig. Ben Zelig."

"*Shalom aleichem a Yid*," the man said in a thickly accented Polish Yiddish. "You and me, we are *landsmen*," he chuckled. Then, he looked at Ben for a long moment and his expression changed. "You are Jewish, right?"

"I'm a rabbi!" Ben said, hating the sound of desperation in his voice.

"Really?"

"You look surprised, why is that?"

"I don't know. You just don't have that rabbi look," Brother Scarsdale said.

The cosmic noose was tightening. Was Ben no longer worthy of that title? "What should a rabbi look like?" he asked.

"Hard to say. A person either has it or he doesn't." Brother Scarsdale stroked his beard contemplatively.

What does that mean? That he once *had* it, but didn't any longer? Or—did he never have it? That was a stab in the ribs.

Sensing Ben's distress, the sexton said, "Pay no attention to me." He tapped his hearing aid over his left ear. "I talk sometimes just to see if I can still hear. So, Rabbi Zelig, are you planning to attend *Shabbes* services at Rabbi Rothstein's *sheel?*"

Brother Scarsdale's Polish-inflected Yiddish made Ben's mouth drop open. What was a *Galitzianer* accent doing in Harlem? That wasn't the only mystery. How could Professor Jacob Rothstein be serving a congregation right here in New York City that no one at the Academy knew anything about?

Ben couldn't summon the courage to ask anything. Instead, he said in Hebrew, "Lead and I shall follow."

Brother Scarsdale didn't appear to understand his Sephardic-inflected Hebrew, so Ben tried in Yiddish. That he understood.

"Your Yiddish has a strong Haitian flavor. Is that where you're from?"

"No. I was born in Ohio," Ben said.

"That must be it," Brother Scarsdale said.

Since he had asked, why couldn't Ben? "Where are you from?"

"I was born right here in Harlem," Brother Scarsdale said, "I learned my Yiddish from Rabbi Rothstein. We all did. He's quite a linguist, you know. Fluent in Hebrew and Polish, translated Shakespeare into Swahili, but Yiddish is his mother tongue. His great-great-great grandfather was Moses Rothstein, the greatest commentator on the Bible since the first Moses. Amazing man, our rebbe." He looked at his watch. "Join me. You're going to love the service and I guarantee you, Rabbi Rothstein's sermon will be one of the great experiences of your life." He put his arm in Ben's, who tried his best to keep up, but his legs were still wobbly as they walked through the brightly lit streets of Harlem.

Along the way Brother Scarsdale paused several times so Ben could rest his aching body. Ben asked a few more questions, but his guide urged him on.

"It's getting late. We can *schmooze* later." Ben stopped to catch his breath. "Please try to keep up," Brother Scarsdale's tone was kindly but urgent.

When they arrived at Temple B'nai Sheba on the corner of 125th Street and Lennox Avenue, Ben was amazed.

"This is the oldest synagogue in New York," Brother

Scarsdale said proudly. "The carved stones were transported from quarries in the hills surrounding Jerusalem." Ben looked at the glass enclosed roster on the large oak door. It read "Senior Rabbi, Doctor Jacob Rothstein." The second line read "Sexton, Brother Abner Scarsdale."

The interior of B'nai Sheba was huge and cavernous. A dome-shaped ceiling featured a purple and gold Star of David. There were hundreds people in attendance, all of them African-American, ranging from youngsters who ran up and down the aisles to young marrieds, middle-aged couples and seniors. The men wore *tallitot*, traditional prayer shawls, and beautifully embroidered *yarmulkes*. Women of all ages were resplendent in their best *Shabbos* attire. Brother Scarsdale offered Ben a *tallit* and *yarmulke* when they entered the sanctuary. On the right side of the ark was an empty throne-like chair topped with a wooden carving of the Lion of Judah, presumably a seat of honor reserved for the rabbi. A choir composed of men in royal blue satin robes, all with matching *yarmulkes*, and women in purple, flanked the Ark.

Brother Scarsdale made room for Ben in the first row among several fashionably dressed, attractive young people who warmly bade him *"A geeten Shabbes."* Again with the Polish accent!

The choir began to sing a rousing rendition of *Shabbat Shalom*, a familiar Sabbath hymn. The beat was a combination of gospel, hora and Hasidic melodies, and the lyrics were in Yiddish instead of Hebrew. The choir was composed of a superb blend of voices and every one of them was clearly moved by the *Shekhinah*, The Divine Presence, as they sang and clapped their hands. The joy on their faces was contagious and Ben began to feel their enthusiasm. When the hymn ended, the congregation remained standing and turned to the main door at the rear of the sanctuary. The choir segued into a slow, melodic chant as the rabbi entered, greeting his flock as he walked slowly toward the pulpit. It was difficult to see him from afar, but when he arrived at the front row, Ben saw that the rabbi, an elderly man in a purple and gold robe, bore an amazing resemblance to *his* Professor Rothstein, except for one thing. He was Black. They had the same soulful eyes, the same flowing beard and white hair curling around the edges of the *yarmulke*, even the same pained, but dignified, gait. So there are two Rabbi Rothsteins! One White and one Black.

"A *geeten Shabbes*," he said to Ben.

His Yiddish was exactly the same Polish-inflected accent as Ben's Rabbi Rothstein! "Were you, by any chance, born in Poland?" Ben asked.

"Yes, indeed," he said, "and many, many generations of my family before me." He smiled broadly. "Many, *many* generations."

"Where in Poland are you from?" Ben was amazed at their vocal resemblance.

"A small village not far from Cracow. Smoloviczi, to be precise. Are you familiar with the history of the Jews in Poland?"

"Obviously not," Ben replied. "How long have Black Jews lived in Poland?"

"Since the early middle ages. Jews from all over the diaspora came to Poland over the centuries and remained. Vikings came and went, as did the Russians, the Germans, the French and even the Turks, but our people stayed, essentially because we had nowhere else to go. Not until America, the *goldene medina*, opened its gates, that is. And now—Israel!"

Ben was overwhelmed. This Rabbi Rothstein had the same radiant smile and speech pattern as *his* Rabbi Rothstein and he had to ask. "Are you aware that there is another Rabbi Jacob Rothstein?"

"Of course," he smiled, "who isn't? Fine man, great scholar, a gift to our people."

"Are you . . . Are you, related?"

"*The same blood courses through both our veins,*" he said in Polish-accented Hebrew. "Brother Scarsdale told me you were a rabbi. Do you have a congregation?"

"Temple Har Zion in Los Angeles."

"Oh? I heard that pulpit was vacant."

A sting went through Ben's heart. What does he know? He was desperate to find out.

"I thought I read in the *Rabbi's Newsletter* that they were looking for a replacement." Seeing the panic on Ben's face, he quickly changed course. "I must be mistaken," he said, "but if you are looking for a change, I am seriously thinking about retiring." As he moved on, he smiled and said, "A *geeten Shabbes* to you once again and welcome to B'nai Sheba."

Ben was obviously in uncharted territory, but it felt surprisingly familiar. When he entered this synagogue he was a complete stranger, but looking around at the worshippers swaying and singing as his people have done for centuries, Ben began to feel like a member of the family.

After a few moments, the congregation settled back and Rabbi Rothstein rose to the *bimah*. He smiled warmly and nodded to his flock. "A *geeten Shabbes,*" he said.

A chorus of voices thundered, "A *geeten Shabbes, Rebbe.*"

The rabbi led them through the first section of the prayer service, and then paused after reciting the traditional prayer that marked the next section. "All rise," he said.

Brother Sexton walked over and opened the Holy Ark.

"And now we come to the *Mi Sheberach*, the prayer for healing. Will the mourners please approach the *bimah*" the rabbi said.

About a half dozen people left their seats and made their way up front. As they passed, Ben noticed a man in an Army captain's uniform carrying a folded American flag and a boy of about six or seven with his father.

"The congregation will please remain standing," Rabbi Rothstein said, "as the mourners recite the timeless prayer our beloved poet, Judah HaLevi, delivered to us in the twelfth century, but whose words are eternal."

Ben vaguely knew the poems of HaLevi, but he had never heard one read in a service.

A young woman was the first to read. "Tis a fearful thing, to love what death can touch."

The rabbi and congregation responded in unison: "Amen."

The Army officer, holding the folded flag under his arm read, "A fearful thing, to love, to hope, to dream, to be."

"Amen," was the thundering response.

The young man and his son held hands as they both recited: "It is a holy thing, to love and to lose. A fearful thing to have loved so completely and oh, to lose so soon . . ."

"Amen."

The final reading was by a middle-aged woman. She held up a photo of a handsome teen-age boy. "Tis a *human* thing to love," she said and raised a second photo of a slightly older boy. "Tis a *holy* thing to love," she said and raised a third photo. This one was of a young man, perhaps in his early 20s. "Tis a human and a holy thing to love what death has touched."

"Amen."

Ben was awestruck. In all his years and in all the synagogue rituals he had officiated or attended, he had never been so moved and he applauded with all his heart along with Rabbi Rothstein and the congregation. *Tis a fearful, holy thing to love what death can touch.* Ben felt tears welling up, but strangely, he was not bereft. He was among the living; those who love and lose and carry on.

The congregation sat down and silence filled the huge sanctuary. "The only thing that transcends death is love," Rabbi Rothstein pronounced. "And what is the engine that drives life and enables us to continue to love?"

There was a moment of silence. Then, the rabbi's voice resounded: "FAITH! Faith is what enables us to continue to glory in the life God has preordained for us. Let me hear my congregation . . ."

"AMEN!" the entire congregation responded.

Slowly, the rabbi put on his reading glasses, opened his Bible and declaimed, "In the thirteenth month of our exile, the hand of the Lord was upon Ezekiel, the son of Buzi, and he said unto him . . ."

Ben suddenly realized that the rabbi's Polish accent was gone. He sounded like Sir John Gielgud!

"Son of man, look heavenward and see the vision I have revealed unto you." Rabbi Rothstein removed his glasses, shook his head, then walked across the *bimah,* stopping several times to look at the ceiling. Finally, he turned to the assembled. "Ezekiel looked, but saw naught. Now, Ezekiel was sorely troubled. The Lord told him that He had just revealed a vision, but the prophet can't see a thing. Sheepishly, Ezekiel asks, 'What vision is that, Lord?'"

Rabbi Rothstein gestured toward the congregation. "'The one I'm revealing to you right now!" He became animated and his demeanor changed again. He was now a fire-breathing preacher, possessed of The Divine Spirit. "'What's wrong with you, Son of Man? It's plain as day!'"

His charismatic presentation gripped Ben like no other preacher ever had. Gone was the Polish-Yiddish inflection, no more Anglo-Saxon deference. Even the fire and brimstone veneer faded and the voice of an Old Testament prophet emerged. "'Help me Lord,' Ezekiel cried out. 'HELP ME, for I see naught.'"

He looked out at the congregation. "What was up with the man? The Lord reveals a vision and his servant Ezekiel can't see it? What's the problem? Doesn't God know how to transmit a clear message?"

"Yes, he does!" The response was unanimous.

"So why couldn't the man see what God was showing him? He was a prophet, wasn't he?"

"That's right! The impassioned response was again, unanimous.

The rabbi walked across the *bimah*, smiling. "It's really simple, if you think about it. You know, you can have the finest TV set money can buy."

The sermon became contrapuntal as the congregation leaned into his rhythm.

"It can be top of the line," his voice developed a deep tremolo.

"Top of the line." the choir was right on beat. "Surround-sound. Flat screen . . ."

He paused and studied his flock for a long moment. "But, I say, I say, but . . ." Rabbi Rothstein's eyes twinkled. "I say—if your set isn't plugged in, you won't see anything at all!"

The enthusiasm was intoxicating.

"The problem wasn't with God. He was transmitting just fine. Ezekiel was the problem. His faith wasn't plugged in and that's why he didn't see anything."

The congregation burst into applause. The rabbi paused

until they fell silent. "So, Ezekiel reached deep into his heart of hearts, then into his soul of souls, until he found the right extension cord, the one called *faith*. He took the initiative, he made the plunge, he leapt the leap and plugged his faith into the living God and behold—the heavens opened up and *all* God's glory was revealed to him in *all* its splendor."

"Praise God," the congregation responded.

Rabbi Rothstein smiled. "Now that's what I call good reception!"

They applauded. The rabbi looked from the congregation to the domed ceiling. He studied it for several moments. "Now, Ezekiel was connected. As soon as he was tuned in, he looked up and what did the man see? He saw a wheel!"

"That's right. That's what he saw. Hallelujah!" the congregation responded.

"I say the man looked up and he *saw* a wheel a-turning. I'm not talking about a dream, here."

"Not a dream," the choir responded.

"Ezekiel looked up and saw a wheel a-turning, way up in the middle of the air. This was no fantasy. It wasn't animation or digital trickery."

"It was for real!" someone yelled loudly.

"That's right! Oops, wait a minute! There's something in that wheel," the rabbi said, looking at the ceiling as though he were narrating an event taking place right there in front of the entire congregation. "It's turning, I tell you. Good God, is that thing ever turning!" He paused to get a closer look. "I see it now. There's a wheel *within* a wheel. That's it. A little wheel inside a big one."

"Praise God!"

"Now, the little wheel's run by faith and the big wheel,

ah, the big wheel's run by the grace of GOD!" He spoke as though the image he was watching was growing larger by the moment. He spread his arms as if to grab the wheel and pull it towards him.

The choir started to sing a rousing hymn and the entire congregation leapt to their feet to join them. "Ezekiel saw the wheel, way up in the middle of the air, a wheel in a wheel, way in the middle of the air."

Rabbi Rothstein took the solo. "The little wheel's run by faith and the big wheel's run by the grace of God . . ."

After an ecstatic rendition of the song, sung over and over, the audience sat down amid "Praise God! Hallelujah!" and a few Polish-accented Yiddish "*o-meyns.*"

When the congregation settled, the rabbi continued. "God is offering us the deal of a lifetime," he said with a broad smile. "It's the best investment you will ever make. He will give you all the grace you can handle provided, ah yes, provided, I say, that you plug yourself in *and* contribute a little faith."

"O-meyn," the congregation was right with him.

"A dollar's worth of grace for a nickel's worth of faith. Nobody can beat that deal, I guarantee it. I say, a dollar's worth of grace for a nickel's worth of faith. Do I have a witness?"

The spirit within Ben cried out. "I'm a witness!" He shouted with all his might. Soon he was joined by an ecstatic throng.

The choir burst into a rousing rendition of a popular Hebrew song with a Gospel beat. "*Heveynu shalom Aleichem, heveynu shalom Aleichem . . .*" *I bring you joy, healing and comfort,* the choir sang. Rabbi Rothstein swayed and danced across the pulpit with his arms raised; his face aglow.

Watching the rabbi's lustrous eyes and radiant face, Ben

felt that his light was beginning to glow. Yes, the very flame of faith that he thought he had lost was now less than ten yards away. Ben was being rejoined with his people through the song. Ben closed his eyes and felt an echo of the rapture that was once his. When he opened his eyes, the rabbi was beckoning Ben to join him on the *bimah*. Ben leapt onto the stage, his wounded legs forgotten. They clasped arms and danced and danced! The movements came from some secret place in Ben's soul and he felt he was being reborn.

He sang out in Hebrew, *"Heveynu shalom Aleichem!"* The heavy depression drained off Ben like so much sludge. He stood before the lectern, looking out at the huge assembly and cried out, "THE LIGHT WITHIN ME SHINETH!"

"Yes, it does!" a chorus of voices joyfully affirmed.

As ben walked from harlem to Morningside Heights, a familiar Psalm wafted into his brain. *He restoreth my soul.* Ben had been granted life's greatest gift. "Truly, God works in wondrous ways," he said gratefully as the gates of the Rabbinical Academy dormitory swung open.

Just as he was falling asleep, Ben heard pounding on the door. "Zelig, for you. House phone!" came the voice of the student from across the hall. Ben pulled himself painfully upright and staggered out the door and down the hall. Who knew he was here besides the rabbi? He picked up the receiver. It was the night watchman. "There's a call for you, Rabbi Zelig. Should I put it through?"

"Who is it?"

"I don't know. Some girl."

Ben felt his heart stop. "Yes, put it through immediately!" He heard a click as the watchman hung up and the line connected. "Lizzy? Is that you, darling? Is everything all right?"

"I'm not your darling, you son of a bitch!"

Ben clutched the phone with two hands. "Naomi?"

"Yes, Naomi, dipshit."

Ben let out a sigh of relief. "Praise God," he said in Hebrew under his breath.

"How could you pull something this cruel?"

"Cruel? What are you talking about?"

"I don't know how you put them up to it, but this is too much even for a *schmuck* of a rabbi."

"Naomi, how did you find me?"

"You said you'd come to visit my father and my name still opens doors at that banana factory. I made inquiries. So stop with all this stalling bullshit. Who really called to say my father was in the ICU at St. Mark's?"

"Wait. What? Your father is in the ICU? When did this happen?" Fear clutched at Ben's chest.

There was a pause on the other line.

"Naomi?"

"This isn't a scam?"

"What? No. No scam."

"Oh my God. They said he wasn't expected to recover." All of the bluster was gone from her voice.

"Naomi, listen. I've got to get to the hospital. I suggest you do the same." Ben hung up the phone before she had a chance to reply. If his knees still hurt he didn't notice as he raced down the hall.

———————

BEN WALKED THE TEN BLOCKS to St. Mark's Medical Center as quickly as he could. The security guard directed him to the ICU on the fifth floor when he arrived, but he soon learned his mentor was no longer there. The resident on duty explained that Professor Rothstein had been released to a private room.

"We understand that the professor fell in his office and bled profusely, so he's desperately in need of a transfusion, but there's been a complication. I'm so sorry, but he is not expected to recover," the resident said, her voice gentle. "You can go see him. He's on the fourth floor."

Ben walked down the stairs to save time waiting for the elevator and spotted the number the resident had given him. As he pushed the door open, Ben heard a sound coming from behind the curtain that had been pulled around the bed. Cautiously, he peered around it. Naomi sat on a chair holding the rebbe's hand and sobbing. Rabbi Rothstein was pale. Tubes and wires monitored his vital signs. Ben stood behind Naomi for several minutes before she turned to look at him.

Without her makeup and salacious wardrobe she looked like a frightened child. Her face was red and her eyes were swollen. "I did this. It's my fault." She tried to muffle her cries but there was too much emotion to be stifled. Ben couldn't hold back his tears, either.

A nurse came in and asked them to wait in the hall while she performed a procedure. A doctor in a white lab coat followed her into the room. He introduced himself as Dr. Alan Scheins, a specialist in immunology and hematology.

"Hematology?" Naomi asked. "Does he have some kind of blood disorder?"

Dr. Scheins was a middle-aged man who looked much older. He had the demeanor of a research scientist who was more comfortable with microbes and microscopes than he was trying to explain complicated medical diagnoses to patients' relatives. "Please wait outside. I'll be with you presently," he said.

In the corridor outside, Naomi turned to Ben. "He looks so old and frail. He's the only family I have left and I've wasted so much time being angry, making him responsible for all my problems. How will he ever forgive me?"

Naomi started to shake and Ben tentatively pulled her in close like he used to do with Lizzy when she was inconsolable. Naomi stiffened for a moment and then slumped into Ben's arms, weeping.

"Forgive you? You are the light of his life, Naomi! If anything can help him now, it's having you back."

When Doctor Scheins emerged, she ran to him. "What's going on? Is he going to be all right?"

Dr. Scheins explained why he was called in. Apparently, Professor Rothstein had developed a rare blood disease that only appears in certain European Jewish men. It was related to a vestigial gene that became corrupted during the Black Plague that devastated much of Europe in the fourteenth century. Twenty-five million people are said to have died from the deadly bacterium in the first five years of the plague. The best physicians of the time were Arabs and the Jews who lived among them in Spain and North Africa. When the plague struck in Europe, rabbi-physicians from the East sent epistles to the far-flung communities of the Jewish diaspora detailing the methods they had discovered to ward off the deadly contagion. They gave precise instructions on how to concoct a potion that would make them immune to the disease. It worked amazingly well. So well, in fact, that the relative health of the Jews convinced the Christians that the plague was a creation of the Hebrew nation, and they inaugurated a wave of bloody pogroms that resulted in the deaths of tens of thousands of Jews.

"Rabbi Rothstein has the plague?" Ben asked in shock.

"No. I wish that was all we were dealing with here," the doctor said. "We can treat that easily today with streptomycin. The problem is that the powerful medication created by the rabbi-physicians of the time involved the alteration of the gene that made one susceptible to the plague. A lingering side effect is an enzyme released by the corrupted gene that creates anti-bodies in the blood. Over the years, that enzyme became recessive so it's extremely rare to find it manifest so long after it was first introduced, but your people . . ." he looked around. "*Our* people, have carried that recessive gene in the collective pool for the past six centuries. Unfortunately, Rabbi Rothstein inherited that corrupted gene and that's our problem. It's not from the residual effects of the plague, but from a severe loss of blood related to his fall."

"All he needs is a simple transfusion?" Naomi and Ben asked, almost in unison.

"A transfusion, yes. Simple, no. The antibodies created by the corrupted gene are called anti-krell antibodies and they're very potent. Their function is to prevent unfamiliar cells from entering the blood stream. The upside is that Rabbi Rothstein has a powerful immune system. Unfortunately, that's also the downside. When a patient has such strong immunity, his antibodies will attack any foreign substance, including blood, unless it's from a *precisely* matching source. In other words, the only transfusion his body will accept would have to come from a donor with not only the appropriate blood type and cellular structure, but also a history and constellation of matching antibodies. Anything short of that would cause his immune system to attack his body and his organs to shut down."

"Give him my blood, for God's sake," Naomi pleaded.

"If we could, we would, but for whatever reason, that gene appears only in males, which by definition renders you unsuitable. We need an XY marker from a male donor of Jewish descent, who comes from the exact area of Eastern Europe he came from and whose ancestors date back to the fourteenth century making them literally extended family. Unfortunately," he looked at Naomi, "from what I understand, his entire family perished in the Holocaust."

Naomi nodded. Dr. Scheins' eyes rendered the verdict.

"But there's got to be someone, somewhere with a matching set of genes," Ben said. "With all your sophisticated data banks and the Jewish bone marrow registries, can't you . . . ?" Ben wished he knew what to say, what to do. Wished he had listened to his mother and studied medicine.

"We're trying, but finding a match can take a long time and we don't have months. At best we have days before his body starts to shut down and his organs fail."

"No!" Naomi cried.

"Short of a miracle, the prognosis is not good. I'm afraid you'll have to prepare for that." Dr. Scheins looked at Naomi with a gentle expression. "I'm sorry." His phone vibrated. "Excuse me. Dr. Scheins here." He headed down the long corridor, the phone to his ear.

Ben watched him go and then turned. "Naomi . . . ?" Ben wasn't sure what he was asking—or why. He could barely see her eyes; they were awash in tears. "Where did your father come from?"

"A small village near Cracow nobody ever heard of."

"Smoloviczi?"

———

HARLEM WAS ASLEEP. The boisterous crowds that had filled the streets the night before were gone. Ben sat on cold stone steps and stared at the locked doors of Temple B'nai Sheba. He must have sat there for quite a long time because he dozed off. When he awoke, he beheld the most amazing sight. The rising sun appeared to be turning, like a wheel. His eyes burned but he couldn't stop gazing at the sun.

"The little wheel runs by faith and the big wheel runs by the grace of God," someone said. When Ben's eyes adjusted to the light, he recognized the handsome face of Rabbi Jacob Rothstein of Temple B'nai Sheba who stood in front of him wearing a beautifully embroidered *yarmulke*. He smiled and extended his hand, which Ben accepted as he struggled to his feet. "Why have you have come back?" The rabbi asked.

Ben looked into his eyes. "Because I need a dollar's worth of grace."

SEVERAL HOURS LATER, Ben sat in the hospital waiting room holding Naomi's hand as Dr. Scheins came toward them. Naomi jumped to her feet. The doctor shook his head and said nothing for a long, agonizing moment. Then—"It's a miracle!"

Naomi gasped. "He's all right? He's going to live?"

"So far, the transfusion appears to have worked," Dr. Scheins said. "His vital signs are improving rapidly. We're not entirely out of the woods yet, but I'd say his chances of pulling through are reasonably good."

"Oh, thank God," Naomi said, throwing her arms around the doctor, who patted her back awkwardly.

"Thank God, indeed," Ben said.

Naomi turned to Ben. "I owe you an apology. Maybe a dozen apologies after all the things I said. I was horrible to you."

"You owe me nothing. Just make peace with your father."

Tears streamed down her cheeks as she nodded and turned to the doctor. "Can I see him?"

"He's resting, but you can go in. Please keep it calm. He needs to preserve every ounce of energy."

She rubbed her eyes with her sleeve and walked toward her father's room.

The cosmic plan was now completely revealed and Ben couldn't restrain his joy.

"You seem very sanguine," the doctor said. "Do you know something I don't?"

How could Ben explain it? They watched Naomi walk up to her father.

Rabbi Rothstein sat up in bed without tubes or monitoring devices. "Naomi, Naomi, *Or Chayi*, light of my life," he cried and tremulously extended his arms.

"Papa, Papa, Papa." She threw her arms around him, weeping for joy.

Ben turned back to the doctor. "Where is Rabbi Rothstein?" he asked. "The other Rabbi Rothstein, that is, the donor."

"He left shortly after the transfusion," Dr. Scheins said. "He apologized for leaving so abruptly, but he said he was late for his *Shabbos* morning service. Amazing stamina for a man his age. Oh, he did ask me to convey a message. He said congratulations, your investment paid off."

Ben couldn't help grinning.

"Got any tips?" The doctor asked. "I'm in the market, myself."

"I've got the inside track," Ben said. "A dollar's worth of grace for a nickel's worth of faith. It works miracles."

The doctor turned to go, but Ben stopped him. "Excuse me, Dr. Scheins, may I borrow your cell phone?" The doctor handed him the phone and Ben punched in a number.

"Aliza? It's Dad . . ."

ACKNOWLEDGMENTS

With love and gratitude to Meryl Moss and her creative team of editors, publicists and marketing professionals.

To my gifted and patient editor, JeriAnn Geller. It is she who created the magical arc that spans three generations of LOVE, FAITH and a PAIR of PANTS.

Thanks to my daughter, Polly Segal, a talented singer and songwriter whose encouragement guided me through the many incarnations of this book.

My thanks to Janice Lynde, an award-winning actress and best-selling author, whose support and insight helped me tell my story.

My appreciation to Carl Lennertz, mentor and friend.

Last, but definitely not least, my thanks to Bellrock Entertainment, Inc., for their ongoing support.

HERB FREED started his adult life as an ordained rabbi and became the spiritual leader of Temple Beth Shalom in Lake Mahopac, New York, while producing and directing three shows at the Maidman Playhouse in New York City. Eventually, he resigned his pulpit to become a movie director. He has directed and produced 15 feature films most of which have had psychological, spiritual and/or social themes in spite of their commercial categories. He is best known for *Graduation Day* and *Tomboy*, as well as the taut thriller *Haunts*, and *Child2Man*, a story of survival during the Watts riots. He is also the author of *Bashert*, a novel.